To: Sis. Abeete

Thank You!

Enjoy

A. D'Anjou

THE WINDOW

Santita D'Anjou

WESTBOW
PRESS®
A DIVISION OF THOMAS NELSON
& ZONDERVAN

WestBow Press books may be ordered through booksellers or by contacting:

WestBow Press
A Division of Thomas Nelson & Zondervan
1663 Liberty Drive
Bloomington, IN 47403
www.westbowpress.com
1 (866) 928-1240

ISBN: 978-1-5127-0398-6 (sc)
ISBN: 978-1-5127-0399-3 (hc)
ISBN: 978-1-5127-0397-9 (e)

Library of Congress Control Number: 2015911470

Print information available on the last page.

WestBow Press rev. date: 08/17/2015

Acknowledgements

To my Heavenly Father, you never leave me or forsake
me. Thank you for your constant presence with me
every night as I transcribed the story you put in
my heart. Apart from you, I can do nothing.

To my Husband, thank you for your amazing support during
this time. Thank you for giving me time away to write during a
very busy season in our lives. I love and cherish you. We did it!

To my Spiritual Parents, I couldn't have imagined
doing something of this magnitude without your
example and encouragement. Thank you!

For my late Aunt Christine
It brings me great peace and great joy knowing that
you are in Heaven cheering us on. I miss you.

And it shall come to pass in the last days, says God, That I will pour out of My Spirit on all flesh; Your sons and your daughters shall prophesy, your young men shall see visions, your old men shall dream dreams.

Acts 2:17 (NKJV)

Chapter 1

As I leap back into consciousness, the room is spinning. The ceiling swirls in a blue haze. I shake my head so hard to awake from the haunting dream that my head pounds like a bass drum. Sweat trickles down my brow, and it feels as if my heart is beating on the outside of my chest. When I finally gain full capacity of my sight and awareness, I am still afraid it wasn't just a dream. It was so vivid and clear that it felt real. After about a minute or two, my heart stops racing and my breathing becomes normal again.

Right across my room, on my cherry-oak armoire, lays my red, leather-bound journal. I stare at it for a while, contemplating if I should leave the safety and comfort of my bed. There is still a fear of danger even though I have awoken, and no one else is in my room but me. Soon, I muster the courage to retrieve my journal and run quickly over to get it. I dive back into bed and catch a glimpse of the time. It is 3:15 in the morning and nearly time to wake up for school. I decide to go ahead and make my entry now, while the dream is still fresh in my memory. I once was told that writing your dreams down as soon as you wake up will ensure you don't miss any important pieces. This journal is comprised of every dream I've had since I was ten years old. I remember the day my Aunt Destine bought it for me. It was seven years ago.

My Aunt Destine was my favorite person on the whole planet. She was a woman of short stature, but wisdom as tall as the eye could see. She had wide hips, so she rarely ever wore pants because she said they made her look fat or— "as big as a house," as she told me. My Aunt Destine loved food, family, and the Lord. As a child, I remember going over to Aunt Destine's house every Saturday to pick her up. She loved my mom's cooking, so she made it a point to visit every weekend just to get a taste of her famous tuna casserole and homemade sweet tea. She enjoyed spending time with us, and we loved having her company. She was my mom's older sister. After their mother passed away, she had to raise her siblings.

There were only three of them— Aunt Destine, who was eighteen at the time, my Uncle Ale, and Mom, who was only five when their mom passed away. My mom and Uncle Ale never knew their dad, which was a huge part of why Uncle Ale turned out the way he did. Uncle Ale was the middle child, and as the cliché says, he was a little unusual. He was very troubled and tended to stay in trouble after his mom passed. Uncle Ale seemed to never get over it and became an alcoholic as a result. I don't think I can remember him ever being sober. The night he died was horrible for all of us. One cold November night, Aunt Destine, my mom, and I went into town to look for him. Aunt Destine had gotten a call from a close family friend, who told her that he was standing on the corner harassing people for money, so we went out looking for him. We spotted him sitting on the corner of A.L. Greens, which was our neighborhood shopping center. He swayed back and forth on the sidewalk, as he mouthed obscenities at everyone that passed.

"There's that fool," Momma said.

Aunt Destine didn't say a word. Her silence always revealed how disappointed she was in him. She couldn't bring herself to say one negative word about him, but I knew she despised how he had turned out just as much as Momma did. As we sat at the red traffic light waiting to rescue Uncle Ale, I watched him intently. I watched as his head swirled in a circle, as if he had just been spun around. Then, suddenly he collapsed to the concrete, hitting his head on the curb as he fell. The light turned green, and Aunt Destine sped to the sidewalk. In panic, she yelled, "Ale!" My mom was hysterical and couldn't control herself. All she could do was walk back and forth praying to God he would at least open his eyes. Aunt Destine demanded, "Call 911!"

I sat on the cold, hard concrete watching Uncle Ale twitch with what little life he had left in him, until finally the ambulance came. He was in a coma for three days, and on the fourth day, since he wasn't improving, they decided to take him off life support. After Uncle Ale's death, Aunt Destine and my mom were inseparable. They were all each other had left. They both proved to be strong women, because they didn't let his tragic death tear them down.

ᔓ

I would often sit with Aunt Destine just to listen to her talk. She had a peculiar voice. Some might think that means strange, but her voice was far from strange. Her voice was precious. There was something about when she spoke; when she opened her mouth everyone listened. She had a meek and low tone that flowed with nothing but love. It was easy to be around her and listen to her because she always had some words of wisdom or encouragement. The day she purchased my journal wasn't like any other day because this was the day I would share something with Aunt Destine that would change my life.

I had woken up from a familiar dream, a dream that never vanishes, but it always seems to stir me no matter how many times I have dreamt it. The dream is about a girl trapped in a house, from which she makes no attempt to leave. The girl seems to be me, but I can never get a glimpse of her face. It's as if I'm hovering over

3

her, watching her, but as is common in many dreams, you seldom see your own face. She's in an old rickety house with nothing but windows for walls, but they have no curtains. This frightens the girl all the more because there's nowhere to hide. All she can see is forest and bushes, with sounds of nature coming from every direction. The sky is a gloomy gray with a flash of lightning every so often. As the girl observes the view, she is startled by an old man who circling the house. He wears a long, brown trench coat and a tan bowler hat. His long, silvery hair hangs to his shoulders. It's so thin you can see right through it. The old man walks slowly around the house, intentionally, never making eye contact with the girl. She watches his every move, for hours it seems, but he never says a word or looks at the girl. Eventually, he climbs the steps slowly to enter the house, and the girl begins to scream. As soon as the screaming starts, I jump as quickly as possible out of the dream, with a pounding heart and gasping for breath.

"Naomi," my mom yelled. "Breakfast is ready."

I glanced at the clock— eight in the morning. It was Saturday, so I knew we were headed over to Aunt Destine's to pick her up for the weekend. She would spend the whole weekend with us, which was fine by me, and since my dad had just walked out on us, it was fine with my mom as well. Aunt Destine didn't have any children, so she spent most of her time with us, shopping at A.L. Greens, listening to music, going to church, and my favorite—drinking coffee. Boy, could my mom and Aunt Destine drink some coffee, whether it was winter or summer. Aunt Destine loved sharing her coffee with me, and I loved it too. My mom liked her coffee black and bitter, but Aunt Destine made her coffee with three creams and three cubes of sugar, which made it rich and creamy. Before I talked Auntie into letting me drink coffee with them, she would always scold my mom on giving it to me. She would say, "Johanna! You shouldn't give that girl that stuff. It can stunt her growth!" Eventually, I worked her over, and she gave in to my pleading. Our weekends were filled with laughter and good conversations.

Mostly, I told her about my dreams. I dreamt almost every night, and they were always so vivid. What frightened me the most was that they would sometimes come true. She would always tell me that I reminded her of Joseph, who was a prosperous dreamer in the Bible. She would tell me that dreams are windows to our spirits, and if you look long enough, there is always an answer, a warning, or a piece to life's puzzle.

That day, I decided to share my ever-present dream with Aunt Destine. Of course I shared every dream with her, but I had never told her about this one. I must have been too scared or maybe too ashamed to mention it to her. I was ashamed because when you think of it when you are awake it doesn't seem that frightening, but when you are asleep, it is terrifying. *I mean it was just an old man coming in a house*, I would think to myself. *What is there to be afraid of?* I needed to tell her, and I needed guidance and an understanding of why this dream is so consistent. I finally found the courage to tell her, so I waited until my mom had started dinner that Saturday evening and decided to tell her outside on our back porch. It was our favorite place to sit when the sun was setting. On the porch sat an old, rickety, lime green, iron swing my mom inherited from my grandmother. It was so old that it was beginning to lose its hideous paint and you could see the rusted, bright-orange parts revealing themselves. Even though it creaked as you swung in it, it was a sound Aunt Destine and I had developed immunity to. We would sit down next to each other in it to have our chats and sometimes swing until we were both rocked to sleep. The humidity in Georgia, whether spring, summer, or fall, was always frightful; twenty minutes outside and your clothes were sticking to you. A cool breeze was very rare in the early fall, but on this particular day, the breeze was cool, and the open sky gave off this beautiful color of coral and gold. We could sit on the porch bare foot, drinking ice-cold sweet tea for hours until my mom called us for dinner. I looked over at her and finally said what I knew she was waiting for: "Auntie, I had a dream."

Once I finished telling Auntie the dream she just stared at the sky, which is something she always did when I shared a dream with her. She would sit and think before she said anything. Once I asked her why she always did that. I wondered what she was thinking and why it took her so long to respond. She answered, "Well, it's better to be quick to hear and slow to speak." So I knew to wait until she had the right interpretation of what she thought the dream meant. It seemed that an hour had gone by and still there was no response; I didn't know what to think. Was she just as confused as I was? Finally she rose to her feet.

She looked down at me and said, "You want to take a little drive?"

"Sure," I said standing to my feet.

Then looking up at the sky with her big round hazel eyes, she said, "Well, go and get your jacket. The temperature is gonna drop soon. We need to make a stop at A.L. Greens."

I waited in the car while Auntie went into the store. When she returned, I wasn't sure what to expect. She pulled out a brown box, about the size of a greeting card, but it had some depth.

"What is it?" I asked.

"It's something to help you begin to figure these dreams out on your own. I won't be around forever, ya know."

Then she pulled off the lid, and there it was: a shiny, ruby-red book, at least that's what I thought. She told me it was a journal and to write every detail down as soon as I awake from a dream and that this would help me to interpret their meaning. With excitement, I accepted the gift and the instructions she gave me. She was right. From that day forward, interpreting the dreams was a piece of cake, but it did take time. Writing the dreams down wasn't enough, but it was a major part of understanding them. Aunt Destine would sometimes take days to get back to me about a dream, but eventually it only took some quiet time and meditation for me to get the full revelation of what the dream meant.

Even though I admired Aunt Destine and usually heeded her advice, I never had written down the dream about the old man, the girl, and the house with nothing but windows. I was too afraid to recount the details of the dream. Thinking about how I had come to possess this journal of dreams sent several emotions through me— my late Aunt Destine, Uncle Ale, and the absence of my father all now consuming space in my mind. It was now 4:32 in the morning and only twenty-eight minutes before my alarm would go off to wake me up for school. I decided to take the time to finally make the entry that was seven years overdue.

Chapter 2

Once I finish my entry, I trudge across the hall to my bathroom. I examine my tear drop shaped face with ridicule—rubbing my fingers over a few discolorations left from break-outs. Doing this causes me to think of my dad. I am basically an exact replica of him, besides my hair and complexion. My dad is Hispanic and was born and raised in the Dominican Republic. He's a very handsome man with jet black hair, dark thick eyebrows, and heavy facial features. At the age of thirteen, he was adopted by a very loving family. My father loved them very much, but he longed to see and know his biological family in the Dominican Republic. My father's adopted family's last name was Peterson, which is what my dad changed his last name to when he decided to enter the United States Army. He would always joke about how his last name came in handy considering how he became the manager of a well-known Caucasian-owned bank. This was a big deal in the south during the 80's. He obtained this prestigious position a few years after he was honorably discharged from the Army. I was always the apple of my father's eye, or so he said, but eventually the streets and alcohol took precedent of his darling Naomi. After fifteen years of managing Highland National Bank, they defaulted and had to sell the company. My dad was laid off and my mom assumed the position of the bread winner for our family. Alcohol and other women became my dad's safe haven. Many nights my dad would stay out to the break of dawn the next day, drinking and living it up with his buddies. Through it all my mom remained faithful, until one day she received a mysterious phone call from another woman. That phone call changed her life forever.

ॐ

Johanna Jackson is my mom's maiden name. She was the daughter of an African American bricklayer and a Caucasian stay-at-home mom. Although my mom's mom was a white woman, my mom looked more like a light skinned African American. Once I asked her how could this be, and she responded with a grin, "Well, my dad was as dark as the night's sky. I guess his genes out did my mother's." This made a lot of sense because looking back at photographs, I can admit, my grandfather was a *dark* man. My mom always stuck with the black side of her culture because she grew up around her dad's family. Her mother's family was so bitter about her marrying my grandfather that they disowned her and never spoke to her, which is why I never knew that side of my family. Well, my skin is a mix of all of those cultures and my hair as well, which frustrates me at times. Some days I don't know who I am because I feel like three different people stuck in one body. I towel dry my face and move on to my untamed coils of hair. I decide on putting it in my usual style of a high pony tail with a few stray coils hanging down in the front and in the back. When I walk out of the bathroom to get dressed I hear my mom stirring in her bedroom, so I tip-toe around my room stumbling every so often, trying very hard not to wake her.

The exhaustion from the night was tormenting my eyes during fifth period, which caused Ms. Rayburn to shout my name from across the chemistry lab. Chemistry was one of those subjects that I could definitely do without, but in order to graduate I needed to take Ms. Rayburn seriously. This task alone is very difficult, seeing that she dresses as if she is going to a three ring circus. She is a walking rainbow with no indication of how ridiculous she looks. Ms. Rayburn wears the most uncoordinated clothes and in some weird way, it's as if she enjoys the laughs she hears as students walk by her in the hall. She just holds her head high and glances in their direction with so much confidence that the laughs are silenced within seconds. She recently dyed her hair a rusty orange color, so as she walks toward me it takes little to no effort to snap out of my daze and give her my undivided attention.

"Miss Peterson," she says in her thick Jamaican accent. "Would you like to address the class on how covalent bonds are different from incovalent bonds?"

"Uh…no ma'am. I am sorry, Ms. Rayburn."

I apologize promptly, hoping she would stop with the questions.

"I'm awake now and it won't happen again."

I learned long ago that it is always better to be polite to your superiors and not to mouth off, to forsake embarrassment. Most likely they will lay off if you admit you're wrong and apologize which always works in your favor.

"Sure, Miss Peterson, I expect your undivided attention for the remainder of this period. Is that understood?" she retorts.

I straighten up on my stool to quickly jot down the notes that I missed while I was day dreaming and reply, "Yes Ma'am, I understand."

And off she trots, with no more strange inquiries about ink bombs and cover bombs. Soon chemistry class was over and my day starts to get a little better when I lay eyes on Daniel, patiently waiting at my locker. Daniel has been my boyfriend for two years. We met when I was fifteen at a youth skiing trip I attended with my best friend Emmy. At first I didn't like him and thought he was a geek, considering how he stared at me the entire trip with a geekish grin on his face. After several gifts of admiration and months of flattery, I decided to go out with him. Even then I still didn't like him, but after a year or so, he kind of grew on me. Daniel is 5'5, only an inch taller than me, with sharp gray eyes and golden straw-like hair. He is medium build, but walks with the confidence of a bodybuilder. His ambition is to make it on the US Olympic wrestling team, so he works hard to stay in shape. He is not a materialistic person and attempts to make that clear by his chosen wardrobe. When he arrives at school he looks as if he threw on clothes that were straight from the laundry basket—the dirty laundry basket. At first this was hard to get used to, but as I said before, he grew on me. Although I love him, at times I feel as though I am not *in* love with him. I feel the steam of guilt rising whenever the thought, *Daniel loves me more than I love him*, presents itself. But, it's true. His actions speak volumes louder than his words. One time, three weeks after we started dating, he called me to talk and I mentioned that my phone may be turned off because my Mom and I didn't have any money to pay the bill. He hung up with me and within thirty minutes he was at my front door. I was confused, scared and surprised, all at the same time, because it was late and he knew my mom didn't allow me to have company that late. Out of breath, he told me he ran over to give me the money for the bill. The scary part was, in the middle of winter, he literally ran from his house to bring me the money, which was six miles away. I realized how much I loved him after our first break up. We separated for two weeks because of an argument we had been having about his wandering hands. He would argue for hours about how much he loves me and how he wants to show me his love, but in my eyes, there was no justification for his behavior. I explained to him how that was not something I'm ready for and don't intend on being ready for until I'm married. Then I told him that we needed some time apart, so I could sort through my feelings for him. This confession sent him in a rage, which brought out a side of him I had never seen before. He punched a hole his bedroom wall to show me just how angry he was. His reaction scared me so bad that I told him that it was over and to find someone else he could manipulate to "*love*" him the same way he wants to be loved. I felt a huge relief, because I thought this could be a clean get away. My way out of something I felt was truly a mistake to begin with. A week went by, and I was sincerely hurting on the inside. He called every day, but I stood my ground and never answered the phone. We would pass each other in the hallway, but I would try my best not to make eye contact. Daniel would make every effort to get my attention. Sometimes he would walk by just to touch me, even if his class was in the other direction. When he walked by, he would touch my hand ever so slightly as he passed, sending chills down my spine, ensuring me that I still had feelings for him. The day I realized I wanted him back was the day I saw him with another girl. They were laughing and smiling in each other's faces. It was innocent banter back and forth, but I hated the sight of him laughing with another girl, especially with that look in his eyes, the look of lust, endearment and admiration. This was something I felt only we had shared, something I felt was sacred. I ignored him as usual and continued talking to my friend Emmy, acting as if I didn't notice his new friend, but as I walked by he pulled me by my arm, close enough to his face that I could feel his steamy breath on my ear and he whispered, "I need you." I went home that evening crying. I couldn't eat and was beginning to lose a lot of sleep since all of this had occurred. I had become accustom to him being around: watching T.V. while my mom prepared dinner, finishing homework, going to see the latest movies together, and most of all, sharing my dreams with him. It was tough, but by the end of the second week his calls stopped and this actually scared me, which prompted me into calling him. He picked up on the second ring.

"Hey, baby," he said, as if two weeks hadn't passed and we had never broken up.

"Hey, what are you doing," I replied with little to no reaction to his congenial greeting.

"Just sitting here thinking about you," he paused for a moment and when I didn't say anything he continued, "I miss you so much and I'm so sorry I..."

I stopped him before he could say anything else because I just wanted the pain to end. I wanted him to come over immediately and hold me so that all of this could go away and my heart could feel whole again. After twenty minutes of mushy talk and apologies, that is exactly what he did. Since the breakup we have had minor disagreements, but for the most part he has managed to keep his hands from wandering and respects my wishes—most of the time.

❧

When I reached the locker, Daniel seemed to be preoccupied with another one of those freaky magazines about premonitions.

"Hey, babe," I said as I gave him a peck on the check. Without even looking up from the magazine he replies, "What's up?"

I believe in being able to see visions of the future and prophesy, but this particular magazine obscures everything that is true and holy about prophesy. Once they had an article about a woman who said she knew when the world was going to end. She described the vision in detail saying that the date was painted in red, on houses, on the ground, in the sky, and even on people's foreheads. "The day of the end is coming," she said, "and it is March 30th, 2030." Well, the date came and many people were so frightened that they boarded up their homes and went underground. Some people were so petrified that they began committing suicide and murdering their families. Their justification was written in suicide notes, saying that they didn't want to suffer and they didn't want their families to suffer either. Hundreds of people died that day and the days leading up to that historic event, so from that moment on, I discounted every story they published. Daniel never found an interest in the magazine until we met and I began telling him my dreams. He became even more interested when my dreams began to come true. Although I share my visions with Daniel now, he wasn't the first.

Soon after Aunt Destine died I started dreaming even more, having three, sometimes five, dreams a night. I wrote down every one of them and I noticed that things would happen in my life, in my friend's lives, and in my family's lives, right after I dreamt it. It became so frightening that I had to share this with someone, and since Aunt Destine wasn't here anymore, the first person I confided in was my best friend Emmy. We met in seventh grade, but at first we steered clear of each other because it didn't seem that we had anything in common. One day after P.E. as I entered the locker room, I heard some ruckus in the very back by the showers. I walked toward the back in a hurry to see what was going on. All of the girls were in a formed circle, watching as the bully of the school, Rhonda Pierson, cursed out a scrawny red head. I watched her eyes tear up as Rhonda poked her thick index finger in her face and gave her a detailed description of what she wanted to do to her. When the tears finally fell from her eyes, I couldn't take it anymore. I pushed my way to the center of the circle and stood right in front of the scraggly girl so I was face to face with Rhonda. Everyone was afraid of Rhonda, but not me. I knew her bark was louder than her bite, and she knew that I wouldn't budge, no matter how many threats she barked out. She backed away slowly, laughing, as if I was a joke. As she backed away, the crowd slowly dissipated until there were only the two of us left in the locker room. I handed her some tissue. "Here, wipe your eyes. She's not going to bother you anymore."

She thanked me gingerly, and then we both sat there taking in the silence. I stayed with her until she was ready to face our peers again. From that moment on, we have been inseparable. Emmy has been with me through everything: deaths, divorce, and heartbreak. Her life has always been the epitome of what I wanted my life to be like. Her parents never fight, at least while we are around. Their love for each other is what people only dream of. What amazes me most is that they are still together. Along with the perfect parents, she has an older sister she can confide in and an older brother who protects her. She's smart, kind, very determined to get what she wants, and gorgeous. I have always envied Emmy's flowing red hair paired with her bright green eyes. Not like my thick, frizzy coils and sharp dark eyes. She has a body like a model and can fit into anything she tries on, but I am thin on the top and curvaceous at the bottom. This makes it hard to find clothes that fit me just right. Although she always manages to make me feel good when she compliments my features, deep inside I know she means it, but it doesn't change how I see myself. She always says, "Girl be quiet, I wish I had your butt—you make any pair of jeans look good." I love Emmy and sometimes I feel like she is the only person that gets me. We plan on moving to Atlanta together to attend college in the fall. Hopefully I can hold up my end of the bargain, if Ms. Rayburn doesn't have anything to say about it.

Once I met Daniel, I had two people I could reveal my dreams to who wouldn't think I was crazy. Some of my dreams I haven't shared with anyone, such as the window dream, which is what I have decided to call it. When I have these types of dreams—the ones that are recurring—for some reason I know these particular dreams aren't meant to be shared. There is something that I am not understanding to cause the recurrences, and there's no use in sharing them with someone else if I am not fully getting them myself.

"Any earth shattering prophesies I should be aware of?" I finally inquired, after retrieving my jacket from my locker.

"Well, none as convincing as yours," he replies. "You know I think you should publish some of your dreams and prophesies, Naomi. People need to know that there are some real premonitions out there and that they need to be taken seriously. No one really knows the day or the hour of when the world will end, but they need to know it is inevitable and there are some things they need to do to prepare."

"Okay, so you think that we need to prepare for the apocalypse? Wow, you're hilarious."

He closes the magazine, and leans up against the locker, "Well, we can't just wait around doing nothing, Naomi. We need to have a plan."

With a serious tone I retort, "Here's my plan: to live my life for God and steer clear of as many false prophesies as I can. This is the only way to prepare for the end." I close my locker calmly and head for my next class and continue, "Daniel, you cannot prepare for something like this, but what you can do is hope you are not left behind when all hell breaks loose, literally."

"What do you mean left behind, you going somewhere?" he chuckles foolishly.

He laughed as if I was telling him a joke or trying to tickle his fancy. When it comes to spirituality Daniel is like a polar bear on a beach. He is what people call an agnostic; he doesn't believe in anything, which is what I believe is missing from our relationship. It's hard to communicate with him when it comes to my deepest feelings and what I value most in my life, because he has no concept of what I build my life on. My Aunt Destine called it something in particular. She told me once that my mom and dad were "unequally yoked," and that's why their marriage didn't work. When I inquired about what that meant she told me that when two people are in a relationship together and they have two separate beliefs they are like night and day—oil and vinegar—they cannot coexist together. When she put it like that, I completely understood. I just looked at Daniel and for the thousandth time since we have been together I thought, *what am I doing?* Another setback with this relationship is that Emmy and Daniel hate each other with a passion. She also thinks we are a mixed-matched couple that is going one hundred miles to nowhere. I hardly ever spend much time with her because she cannot stand to be in

Daniel's presence. In his case, he loves to get on her nerves and is intrigued by how fast he can make her disappear when, by some miracle, we all run into each other in the hallway, at school, or the library on Broad Street. Emmy does a good job in dodging us most of the time, but I miss her so much these days. She doesn't have a boyfriend, at least as far as I know, because she is really focused on school and trying to get into the best college Atlanta has to offer. My hope is that I at least graduate.

ॐ

That afternoon, Daniel came over and stayed until night fall. My mom didn't feel so good so she spent most of the day lying down while I catered to her every need. Daniel sat and watched television while I purposely ignored him. Soon he finally got up to leave, but before he left he pitched his genius idea once more as he walked toward the door.

"Come on, Naomi. Think about what I told you. You can't have been given this gift for nothing. Don't you think *your* God gave it to you for a purpose?"

I retort, "I'm sorry what you think is a *joke* I feel is a very serious matter. These aren't just dreams to me; they can really affect the people that I reveal them to."

"Who said it was a joke, he is *your* God, right?"

I open the door so frustrated and eager for him to go home. He walks out and turns around anticipating my response. I poke my head across the thresh-hold and kiss him lightly on his cheek. I reply, "Sure Daniel, see you tomorrow," and closed the door. I lay in my bed looking up at the ceiling wondering how I got myself so deep into something that I know is going nowhere. Then, a million thoughts begin to rush through my head about the day; the journal entry I made this morning and how I still didn't have an interpretation of it, my lackluster day at school, my mom once again, lying in bed all day, and then reverting back to my dead end relationship. Soon I drifted off to sleep. As I floated down into a deep slumber I found myself in a mist of soft pink and lavender clouds. I hovered over a girl who was gazing out into a morning horizon from a balcony which over looked the entire world. Not only were the clouds many different shades of pinks and purples, the sky gave off a stunning hue of the two colors. Then, all of the sudden as the clouds drifted to the west, a huge analog clock appeared in the middle of the sky. It struck twelve and a loud gong shook the foundation of the earth and lines of people appeared just at the base of the clock. They were cascading throughout the earth and sky as if they were waiting on something big. Some people where clothed in robes that gave off a brilliant light, but others wept and wore black garments, which did not give off any illumination. I continued to hover over the girl as she watched all that appeared before her and suddenly realized the girl was me. Once this realization came, I glided into the body which was my own and immediately I became part of the line of people numbly walking toward the clock. As I stood there, I got closer and closer to the front of the line and could see seven large beings taking each person to a room that was closed off from everyone else. They would lift what looked like a drape, but was as thin as a bride's veil, although you couldn't see through to the other side. This was very bizarre and at times I found myself straining to see the peoples' silhouettes once they had crossed over, but there was nothing. This fabric was somewhat like the fabric the large beings wore. It was lightly draped on their huge bodies and hung to the glass bottom floor. Their clothing shone just like the drape that separated our world from their world. The beings were beautiful, so beautiful it was difficult to behold them for too long. Their hair was like silk and the color of amber. Their eyes were as bright as the sun, which explained some of the difficulty in looking at their beautiful faces.

When I reached the head of the line, one of the angelic beings took me by the hand very gently and said, "This way." As

I walked I realized he was taking me behind the veil. I became very preoccupied with the thought of leaving Daniel and not wanting to leave without saying goodbye. I panted with anxiety as we got even closer to the veil. I couldn't walk anymore because now I was crying and I knelt down on the floor, collapsing into a fetal position. My escort turned to me and picked me up with such ease. It was as if he knew my thoughts because his words were, "Now, now—no more tears. I will make sure you get to say goodbye." His voice was so endearing and each syllable brought me peace. For some reason I felt that I knew his voice or maybe had heard it before. He was so familiar to me and I felt safe to be in his arms. There was reassurance that he was going to allow me to say goodbye. Just as he finished his sentence a device that resembled a telephone appeared. He handed it to me and as soon as I put it to my ear I could hear Daniel say, "Hello."

"Hello, Daniel?" I say with a sob.

"Hey babe, what's up?"

With passion and regret I reply, "I just wanted to tell you," I pause for a moment, sobbing into the receiver, "to tell you…that I love you."

"Okay babe—I—I love you too."

"Okay, hon I—I have to go now."

"Sure babe, talk to you soon, good—bye."

"Goodbye."

I hang up the phone feeling rejuvenated, like a huge weight has been lifted from my shoulders. I stood up straight and felt like I had the strength to move mountains. I looked at my familiar companion and he smiled as if he could feel the fire that had just been set inside of me. I returned his smile and said, "I'm ready now."

Chapter 3

The next morning, I immediately recall every detail of the dream in my journal. As I write the words I feel a panic sweep over me. What did this dream mean? Did it mean that Daniel and I are going to break up? Did it mean that I'm going to die? Having the gift of being able to see the future is not always fun because sometimes the dreams are not so favorable and can be difficult to deal with. In the past I have had premonitions that didn't come to pass or maybe they did come to pass, but not how I expected. Once I dreamt that I locked Daniel out of my house while it was pouring down raining. He beat and beat on the door yelling viciously at me, but I would never let him in because for some reason I was very angry. After writing it down, I took one of those long pauses that Aunt Destine used to always take and an interpretation came to me. The rain signified trouble and despair, which is what I have been continually going through since I decided to commit to a relationship with him. Locking him out of the house is a metaphor of how I am really keeping him out of my heart. I love him, but I cannot fully trust and give my whole heart to him because we are not on the same level mentally, emotional, or spiritually. His beating on the door was a sign of the anger that is built up inside of him. Daniel has had a rough life and sometimes he can become very angry. My dreams all have meaning, but it's a matter of taking the time to seek God for what each part means. After much thought, I still didn't really understand last night's dream and decided to go ahead and get ready for school.

The school day was moving along pretty well until I entered Ms. Rayburn's class. She was wearing the most awful outfit that I wouldn't have ever fathomed any human being wearing. The minute I crossed the threshold of the classroom I noticed her neon orange army boots, the red and green flannel skirt that draped to the middle of her shin and the powder blue lace blouse that hugged her round belly. She looked strangely at me. I stood there shocked at the horrific mess she had made of her ensemble today. This shouldn't have come as a surprise to me but it did, maybe because I had never seen her make such a mess of herself. Finally, I took my seat, eyes locked on Ms. Rayburn as she trotted to the board undaunted by the laughs and whispers of the students. "Okay, class—settle down. Today, we will discuss…" and at this point of her sentence I zoned out, daydreaming about my dream. When class is finally over I quickly grab my things and head for the door. Just as I reach the door she calls my name from the back of the room.

"Miss Peterson, can you stick around for a little while?"

With frustration in my voice I reply, "Sure, why not."

Rolling my eyes, I sit down my things and Ms. Rayburn collapses at her desk. I realize that this is the first time I have ever been alone with her and this close. This makes me very uncomfortable because the weirdness she projects from her appearance was even more petrifying up close.

"Miss Peterson, I wanted to inform you that I am fully aware of your distractions in my class. You are missing key information for the final exam and I need you to focus in on my lectures if you want to pass."

"Yes, I know, Ms. Rayburn; I do apologize for being distracted in your class. It's just that—well—never mind."

She leans forward with anticipation of what my excuse is, "No, please continue Miss Peterson."

Making no eye contact, I continue, "Well, I have a lot going on right now and it's kind of hard to explain."

"No need. I am fully aware of what the issue is and my advice to you is to be watchful."

"Watchful? What do you mean?" At this point I am looking her in the eyes.

"Don't be disturbed by sudden events that are going to happen in the near future. Just know, if you remain watchful you will survive."

Perplexed at the conversation, I remained seated.

"No disrespect, Ms. Rayburn, but can I ask what in the world you are talking about?"

She stands to her feet, walks around to the front of her desk and sits on the edge of it, "You are a dreamer, right?"

With confusion and hesitation, and with awareness that she is now three feet away from me, I reply, "Right."

"And your main distraction in my class is probably the dream you had the night before, right?"

"Right," I mumble out.

"Well looks like I am on the right track and have something very important to share with you. I am what you are, a dreamer, a visionary, a seer; whatever you choose to call it. I have had nearly five decades to perfect my gift and have the ability to interpret them as well. This gift is far more important than you realize, and I feel its time you take it more seriously."

Without thinking and without hesitation, I retort, "I do take this seriously." She folds her arms as I continue, "How did you know these things?"

With a sly smirk she replies, "I discerned it. I know a dreamer when I see one—always daydreaming, doodling in a notebook, falling asleep in class, and the most obvious characteristic—biting your nails. You remind me so much of myself when I was your age."

I am incapable of controlling my facial expression at the sound of her last comment, so I look away and respectfully say, "Please, Ms. Rayburn, don't compare me to you, it's too flattering."

Obviously not catching on to my sarcasm she says, "I am only stating the facts, am I not?"

"You are right, I do bite my nails and find myself falling asleep in your class, but these are all characteristics that you can find in any high school student, so that's not a fair observation."

"You are right Miss Peterson, but nobody day dreams for an entire class period without flinching, which is what you did today. And, I have seen that journal you sometimes pull out to look in. You're trying to get the interpretation during your chemistry class!" I hang my head, ashamed of the truth. Ms. Rayburn walks over to me and pats me on the back. "It is fine, Miss Peterson, I am just glad I finally got the nerve to expose the secret I have been keeping from you about my premonition. I have dreamt of you, and from what I have seen, you have a rough road up ahead. My assignment is to tell you to pursue wisdom, be watchful, and steer clear of the tower."

With all of the respect thrown out the window, I yell, "What!?"

She repeats calmly, "Pursue wisdom, be watchful, and beware of the tower." And just like that she drops out of what seems to be a trance and says, "Good day, Miss Peterson."

I stand there stunned and frustrated that Ms. Rayburn feels that she can share something like this with me when we barely know each other. As I slowly walk to the door with thousands of questions racing through my head, she makes one more comment.

"Don't be afraid of your dreams, embrace them. Cultivate the gift that has been given to you."

Even more freaked out by her than I was before, I leave without a single word.

Chapter 4

Without a thought or reservation of being caught for cutting school, I walk out the front door like a zombie. I am so tormented by everything that has been going on lately, I decide to walk home. As I walk, I think about Daniel, how I love him so much, but also how we have almost nothing in common. My mind then wanders to my late Aunt Destine. Oh how I miss her and can really use her advice right about now. My mom being on the brink of a severe depression isn't much help and I would hate to bombard her with all of this, seeing that I am the only stable person in the house these days. Then, I finally dare to reflect on Ms. Rayburn's advice and her unexpected discovery of my misdirected attention in her chemistry class. I turn the corner of Broad Street and decide to hide out in the library Daniel and I always escape to. We spend hours in this library when we just want to sit and read a good book, or in his case, *The Spark: Chronicles of Supernatural Findings*. With little to no one on the streets at this time of day, I stealthily look around hoping no one will notice me. Usually the streets are gridlocked after 4pm, but since it is only a little past noon, the streets are bare, with the exception of a mom strolling her baby and a few business men in fancy suits. When I walk into the two story marble building, I think, *oh how I hope the usual evening and weekend librarians aren't working.* It would be just my luck for one of them to call me in to the principal's office and I get taken back to school. I would be useless in class right now. When I enter the library, a sigh of relief sweeps over me, and I feel at ease. I don't recognize any workers, so the coast is clear to settle here for the remainder of the school day. I walk to the back of the library to my favorite plush blue couch and relax my legs on the short burgundy stool that always accompanies it. I lean my head back enjoying the nice warm sun rays shining through the large window that fills my view. I am still repeating Ms. Rayburn's so-called warning in my head: *pursue wisdom, be watchful, and stay away from the tower.* What did all of this mean? I didn't stick around long enough to find out and no matter what, I vowed never to ask her because this is all too creepy to dedicate anymore thought to. I close my eyes and say a little prayer:

> *Lord, please help me. I am so confused and have no idea what is going on anymore. I need you. Please send me a sign or someone who can help me figure out all of this. You tell me what to do and I will do it. If you say let him go, I will. Amen.*

When I open my eyes, a bronzed hair gentleman is staring down at me. Smiling in adoration, he says, "Well that is the simplest, yet most admirable prayer I've ever heard."

He looks to be of the same mixed cultures as me and this intrigues me, but I am too irritated about him eavesdropping on me that I reply angrily, "Well, I don't appreciate you listening and would like for you to stop staring at me like that. It's creeping me out."

"I'm sorry I didn't mean to creep you out. I only stopped to listen because I am so used to people reading and looking for books in the library, and it's not often that I come across someone praying. Are you okay?"

"Yeah," I sit up in the couch and adjust my posture. "I'm fine, now would you just leave me alone." I snap with frustration and embarrassment.

Instead of obeying my orders he sits down right beside me and that is when I notice his dazzling green eyes. They are so stunningly beautiful that they give off a brilliant reflection when the sun hits them just right. Then, I notice his silky bronze hair that cascaded in waves, which compliments his eyes perfectly.

I stare numbly into them as he says, "No, not until you tell me what's wrong. Maybe I can help?"

"You don't even know me, and I don't know you, so why would I tell you anything. I don't talk to strangers."

"Well, I guess I am not a stranger," he checks his watch, "because you have been talking to me for the past two minutes."

A smirk sneaks up on his nicely curved lips. I roll my eyes and uncontrollably a smile rises on my face, as well. "First of all, what's your name?" I ask.

"Joseph, and what's yours?"

With hesitation I tell him, "Naomi." *No last names until I discover he's not a serial killer.*

"Wow, I love that name. Always have, that was my mother's name," still sitting uncomfortably close to me, he gazes off for a slight moment, as if he is ashamed, and then resumes looking at me.

Strangely, I can't force myself to look into his eyes again, it seems too personal and every time we do make eye contact I feel the heat of a blush stirring within my cheeks. I focus in on the book shelves right above his shoulder, trying not to meet his gaze with mine.

I counter his compliment with, "Joseph is a name I have always admired as well."

With a more interested expression, he folds his arms and cocks his head to one side and asks, "Why is that?"

"Are you sure you want to know?" I ask him.

"Yes, I am sure, but wait," he tosses the bag that is on his back, to the floor, "does it have something to do with a knight and shining armor or something silly like that?"

I smile, "No, I know that name is common to most people, but every time I hear it I think of the biblical Joseph. So, there is actually a deeper reason why I like your name."

Joseph leans forward in anticipation, "Well, in that case please share. I enjoy hearing bible stories."

Surprised at his willingness to hear a bible story because I'm not used to men wanting to hear stories of this nature, I retort, "Really?"

"Oh please, I am always ready to hear something spiritual. After all, we are spirits, who possess souls and we live in physical bodies. We are spirits first and foremost—right?"

Without any control of my cheeks, I feel a cheesy smile creep up on my face. "Yes, that is right." I hang my head, to hide the smile. "Well, to make it even clearer why I like the name Joseph, someone told me once that I reminded them of Joseph."

"Well, I would love for you to tell me why you admire the name Joseph, so please do me the honor."

With delight, I begin the biblical story of Joseph.

Joseph was the son of Jacob, who was the son of Issac. Jacob had tricked his father into blessing him instead of his brother Esau.

Do I need to go into the whole thing of how he tricked him?

"No...no, I think I have read that story before, but please continue."

"Okay."

So Jacob had several sons, and Joseph was one of his favorites because he was born from his wife Rachel. Jacob loved her dearly, but he had another wife.

"Which, I can't remember her name."

"That's fine, I think her name was Leah."

"Right! Wow, I'm starting to think I am wasting my time telling you this story; it seems you know it already."

"Not quite, please continue," he said with a grin.

> *Well, Jacob had two wives Rachel and Leah. He was basically forced to marry Leah, but she bore him several sons and Rachel only bore him two sons. One of those sons was Joseph. Jacob so admired him that he made him a cloak of many colors, which made his other brothers very jealous. They didn't like Joseph because he was favored by Jacob. Their dislike became even stronger when Joseph decided to reveal a dream he had about them. Joseph told them of a dream he had where their stalks of grain bowed to his stalks of grain. They took this as haughtiness and plotted to kill Joseph. They put Joseph in a pit but Reuben, one of his older brothers, convinced them not to kill him.*

"Wasn't there another brother who helped to save his life too?"

"I'm not sure. I'm giving you the short, short version so pay attention."

At this point Joseph shifted in the couch to make himself more comfortable and I began to feel calm and relaxed sitting and sharing this story with him.

> *So, they sold him into slavery instead. Joseph prospered wherever he went and was favored by God. He was a dreamer and could also interpret dreams. He was eventually put in jail because his master's wife threw herself at him, but he refused her. She then lied on him saying that he tried to sleep with her. Once in jail, he still prospered and became the chief overseer's*

*personal attendant. Soon he was summoned by
Pharaoh to interpret a dream, which no one else in all
the land could interpret. The dream was a warning
that famine was coming and the people needed to store
their crops for the days to come. Pharaoh believed
Joseph and placed him in charge of all the land and
food. Soon everything Joseph said came to pass and
the people looked up to him. Joseph eventually married
and had some children but missed his father, Jacob
and his brother Benjamin. Being the chief overseer
of all the crops of Egypt, Joseph's brothers had to come
to see him to attain food during the famine. When
Joseph realized who they were, he tricked them into
bringing his brother Benjamin back with them and
all the while they had no idea that this was their
little brother they had sold into slavery many years
prior. When they brought Benjamin back, Joseph
couldn't take hiding his identity anymore and revealed
himself to his brothers. They were all frightened that
Joseph was seeking revenge, but he told them that it
all worked together for their good because now they
would live and his father would live in result of the
decision they made.*

"Joseph means, 'to prosper,' and it is very significant to me.
Because I was told, long ago, that this biblical Joseph and I
had something in common, I made it a point to find out more
about him."

"What is it that you have in common with Joseph?" he asks.

"Well, he was a dreamer—just like me," At this point I feel
a sense of shyness because I mistakenly tell him something very
personal.

"What do you mean you're a dreamer? Everyone dreams at
some point in their lives, it's a natural thing."

"Yeah, that's true," I exhale, contemplating if I should continue this conversation. I look up at him, his round face, and his smooth, bright complexion. He is strikingly handsome and his eyes speak to me, without him uttering a word.

I continue, "Sometimes people can't remember their dreams, which happens on occasion, but since I was a child, I would dream three, sometimes five dreams a night. I wouldn't write them down, but I would remember them and eventually the memory of them would fade away. One day my Aunt bought me a journal and told me to write them down so I would not forget them," I pause again, still somewhat embarrassed of how candid I'm being with a stranger.

He fidgets and says, "Please—continue. I know there's more you want to say."

"Since then, I have recorded every dream. Sometimes the dreams I have actually become a reality after I have dreamt them. Not all of them come true, but they all do have meaning, or a warning hidden deep within them."

"Wow, I guess that is unique," now he pauses for a moment and scratches his head. "Could this be what you were praying about? I mean did you have a dream that you are concerned about?"

"Yeah, a dream I had last night is part of my agitation, but there are other things that have conspired the last few days."

I sit idle for a moment contemplating if I should tell Joseph about my dream. He seems so endearing and easy to talk to. *But, I just met him*, I tell myself.

Joseph sits forward again, with his hands clasped together, smiling from ear to ear, looking like he is ready to do a science experiment, "Do you want to share? I am good with solving problems."

At this point I have a flashback of last night's dream— of me saying "goodbye." I reply, "No, I'm fine. I think I can figure it all out on my own."

His grin fades and he says, "Have you ever heard the story of the man who was stranded on an island and didn't have any water to drink?"

"Yes," and I glance at him sharply, "I know where you are going with this."

"Well, I'm going to tell you the story anyway," He grins and scoots closer to the edge of the chair. "This man decided he was going to pray for help and as soon as he finished, a man on a boat came along and offered him a ride to the nearest town." He sits back, folds his arms across his chest, and asks, "Now do you know what this man's reply was?"

I roll my eyes and breathe out a "Yes," through my teeth, but he continues anyway, as if he didn't hear me.

"His reply was, 'no I am waiting on God'." He unfolds his arms, sits back in the chair and finishes with, "Eventually that man died."

I look back over at Joseph, feeling like I have known him forever at this point. He starts to laugh sheepishly and he returns my stare, so I ask, "So what does this have to do with me?" as if I didn't know.

With a flick of his collar and an arrogant tone, he responds, "You asked for help and here I am, offering my expertise."

"Well, what makes you think God sent you?" I retort.

"I don't know, but it wouldn't hurt to trust that notion, would it?"

Playing hard to get is something I am good at, without having years of practice under my belt. Deep down I truly want to share my problems with Joseph, but it's hard trusting someone you just met. Then I realize that, hey, I may not see this guy ever again anyway, how much damage could it possibly do? I straighten up on the couch and turn to face him. He mimics my body language and there he is, face to face with me, and attentive to my every word. This time I meet his gaze for a brief moment and do not fight it. I pull out my journal to read him the dream I had the night before, but before I could read the dream I had to tell him about Daniel. I had to tell him how much I love this boy and I can't seem to let him go. Then I went on to tell him about my struggles with Daniel and how we have different moral beliefs. Finally, I tell him about Ms. Rayburn and the warning she had just given me. He stares off into space just as Aunt Destine would do before she gave me an interpretation. Once it seems that he has an interpretation, Joseph begins speaking:

"That dream is powerful and can have so many meanings, but I think it means that you and this Daniel character will say goodbye soon, like your relationship is coming to an end."

I hang my head, "Oh—I—kind of thought of that too but…"

"You don't want to accept it, just like you didn't want to accept it in the dream. You had to say goodbye before you actually let go?"

Now Joseph has a harden look on his face and he seems more serious than I have seen him this entire time.

"Yeah, but it kind of gave me the impression that I was in heaven, so I…" I pause, not wanting to say what I was thinking out loud.

Joseph's eyes widen, "You think it means…you are going to d-…"

I slide forward quickly and put my hand over Joseph's mouth, "Shhhhhh, don't say it. And you're being too loud," I say with irritation in my voice, "We are in a library, remember?"

I remove my hand from his mouth. Surprised at my friendly gesture, he smiles and I feel goose bumps starting to rise on my arms.

I sit back in the couch and continue, "You can't say that kind of stuff out loud!"

"What's the big deal?" he asks.

"Life and death are in the power of your tongue. I can speak life or I can speak death, so I choose to believe the positive outcome. I don't believe God would give me a dream about my death, so I think you are right about its meaning." At the thought of leaving Daniel, my stomach turns a summersault. With fear and sadness pooling in my heart, tears begin to fill my eyes. Joseph reaches over to touch my hand.

"You are right, our words do hold a lot of weight. Don't cry, Naomi," he says with such empathy.

"It's just he is all I know. I love him and it hurts too much to even think about being without him."

"Well, who knows, it may just be a warning."

He pauses and sits back in his chair again. I wipe a few tears away and look over at Joseph. "What are you thinking now?"

He looks at me, "Do you really want to know?"

"Yes, I do."

His serious demeanor returns. "It seems to me you are looking for someone to fill a void and not a true soul mate. It's dangerous, Naomi. You have so much to look forward to; don't waste your time on something you know is going nowhere."

I sit speechless taking in every word. Thinking about how much the dream makes sense, now that Joseph has vocalized everything I tried so hard not to think or say. All I needed was for someone to say it out loud, for someone to tell me what I had been thinking all along. But, the reality of it all is too much to deal with right now.

"What about the scenery? Why did it seem like judgment day?"

"I will have to think on that one, Naomi. That's a piece I am not clear on. This Ms. Rayburn though, she sounds kind of kooky, but she may be on to something. Don't discount her advice just because she seems strange. She said: *pursue wisdom*, this could mean to just lean on God and don't rely on your own understanding of situations and circumstances; *be watchful*: this can mean to stay on guard, to be prayerful and not to be distracted; b*eware of the tower*: could signify an obstacle or an actually physical place. I am not sure which one, but if I were you I wouldn't go into any towers anytime soon, " he smiles a little and continues, "who knows, this Ms. Rayburn may be someone you would want to take seriously.

"Ha—ha—ha, very funny. Don't joke about the tower thing. That is what really freaked me out."

With a half-smile, I nudge him with my elbow and I say, "But thanks, Joseph—I am glad I talked to you. Your interpretation was confirmation for what I really already knew. My only question is, how am I going to break this to him, or do I just wait for the inevitable?"

"Just..."

Before he could finish, I snap, "That was a rhetorical question." He hangs his head and laughs to himself as I gather my things and stand up.

"Hey, where are you going? I was just starting to get used to your sassy attitude," he blurts out loudly.

"Shhhhh," I gesture, with my index finger pressed to my lips. Then I whisper, "I have to go figure this all out. Besides, it's about that time for me to be arriving home from school."

"From school? Wait a minute, how old are you?" he asks.

"Now, isn't that a rude question to ask a female? I can't share my age." I pause for a moment, enjoying the silence. "But, I will make an exception if you tell me how old you are."

"Sure. I am twenty-four," he says quickly with anticipation for my reply.

Doing the mental math in my head, I tell him, "Well, you are just about six years my senior."

He gives me one of those sly smirks again, which makes butterflies dance in my stomach. "You graduate this year?"

As I pull on my book-bag and tuck my stray curls behind my ears, I respond with seriousness in my voice, "Yeah, trying to, but if I don't clean up my act in Ms. Rayburn's class I am going to have to consider online courses for the summer."

He laughs and helps to fix my book-bag straps on my shoulders, "Well you better get a move on, Miss Peterson."

I snap, "Hey, how did you know my last name? I didn't tell you that." He grabs my shoulders and turns me around.

"If you don't want strange men knowing your name, it's not a good idea to have it embroidered on your backpack."

Feeling like an idiot, I drop my eyes to the floor in embarrassment. I turn back around feeling really juvenile. He lifts my chin and fixes his eyes on mine. He grins at me, and I notice his pearly white teeth that fit perfectly with his charming pink lips. *He's gorgeous*, I think. I fidget out of the position he is holding me in.

Trying not to show my nervousness, I say, "Yeah, my mom gave me this for my birthday this weekend. It wouldn't have been nice to turn it down. I needed a new one badly and this was her way of doing something 'cool' for me. I like it."

"No worries, Miss Peterson," he says as he examines me from head to toe. "Would it be okay with you if I met you here the same time tomorrow, you know, to continue our conversation?"

Without thinking, I say the first thing that comes to my mind, "Well, tomorrow I have school."

"No, no," he laughs out, "tomorrow is Saturday, but good try though."

With a sigh, I say, "We'll see. It depends."

"On?"

"My mood," I say with a blush. Then I walk away, toward the front of the library to exit. Feeling the heat of his stare on neck, I turn around to see if my instincts are serving me correctly. He *is* watching me leave, so I smile and wave goodbye.

ॐ

Walking home, I feel as if I am floating. All I can think about is Joseph and nothing else. His ravishing smile and the way he looked at me with his piercing green eyes is what continues to replay in my head the entire walk home. When I reach my house I realize that I can't even remember one detail of the walk. It is like I walked out of the library and just miraculously appeared on my front door step. I set out to call Emmy as soon as I get in the house—to tell her all about my encounter at the library. I put my key in the key hole and before I can turn the knob, my mom opens the door.

Still in her bathrobe my mom rants out, "Where have you been? I have been worried sick, Naomi! Your sixth period teacher called concerned about you because she saw you during the day and got worried when you didn't show up to class!"

"Mom, my sixth period class is a fluke. All we do is draw fruit and flowers," I say as I throw my backpack on the love seat. "Ms. Rayburn's class is the only class I am concerned about."

She sank down on the couch, to occupy the same spot she has been sitting in, probably, all day. The same spot where the springs have worn and the cushion has sunk in because of the constant occupancy. I take notice of her posture and facial expression, and then it hits me. I feel horrible inside. The Lord knows I didn't want to add to my mom's tormenting thoughts.

"Naomi, please try not to scare me this way," she says with so much terror in her voice.

Of all people, I should know how terrified my mom is of losing someone else she loves.

"Yes ma'am. I'm sorry, it won't happen again." I sit down next to her and hug her as tightly as her frail body will let me.

She has been through a lot: all of her siblings deceased, deceased parents, and after 20 years of marriage a husband that just up and left her with nothing. It was stupid of me not to consider that a school official would call and have her here worrying if I was okay or not. After embracing my mom until she was fast asleep, I slowly stood while guiding her head to the pillow that lay at the end of the couch, pulled a blanket over her, and proceeded to my room. I plop down on my plush bed and all of the sudden, like a tsunami, Joseph comes flooding back into my mind. I decide not to call Emmy and to keep him a secret, just to keep him to myself for a little while. I lie there day-dreaming and replaying our encounter; his kindness, his spirituality, his ability to tell me the truth without reservations and of course, his heavenly face. Joseph was the encompassing splendor that saturated my soul until I drifted off into a deep slumber.

Chapter 5

My heels click as I run down a beautiful corridor. The walls are made of the beautiful Japanese stone, jade. There are columns every five feet and they extend as high as the heavens. I slow my pace for a moment to marvel at the cloudless sky. The sky is a soft orange and a calming pink, and the sun is just touching the edge of the earth. I am in a building which is even more beautiful because of the sunlight that shines through the roofless fixture. The columns are made of pure gold and the floor is also made of jade which is polished so well, you can see your reflection as clearly as you would in a mirror. The floor is waxed to perfection and I am amazed that I can keep my balance. As I continue running, I notice I have on a long ivory gown with gold, silk trimming. The train on my gown is maybe 20 feet or more, so I have to hold it in my hands to keep from tripping. This corridor seems to go on for miles until I finally reach my destination. I run into his arms relieved and tired. He holds me with so much strength and contentment that I can't help but feel safe and secure. He pulls back from our embrace to say, "I love you, Naomi, and no matter what, I will never let anything happen to you." The man in all ivory holds me even tighter, then embraces me once again and we begin to float into the orange and pink atmosphere, spinning ever so slowly, until we reach the sun and saturate its light.

Ring—Ring—Ring—Frustrated, I slap the alarm clock, turning off the annoying buzz. Then I jump up in horror, only to realize I had done it again. Every so often I wake up in a panic on Saturday thinking it's a school day. After coming to my senses and getting over my frustration at my absentmindedness, I settle in my bed to do my usual exercise of trying to remember what I dreamt that night. It sometimes takes me five to ten minutes of lying there in silence for the dreams to come flooding back. Then it hits me that I had an awesome dream. Images begin to fill my mind, contorted images of the breath-taking corridor, the massive columns, the stone walls and *him*. Who was he? I can't bring back the memory of his face. All I can recollect is a blurred image of a male figure. I can't even remember what his voice sounds like, but I do remember comfort and security beaming from his embrace. I remember his words, '*I love you, Naomi*,' and oh how they sounded so real and sincere. Thinking about it gives me goose bumps. I decide to quit trying to make out the face and accept that it was one of those coerced dreams that I have sometimes. I figure, since I fell asleep thinking about Joseph, than maybe it was the primary reason I had a dream about a loving companion. I mean, he is handsome and he does seem to have a relationship with God, which are my top two prerequisites for a mate, now that I know better. On the other hand, he is too old, and who knows, he may be pretending to be a Christian. And, he probably would never think of me in that light. I sit up in bed and reach for my journal, which was not in its usual spot. Then it dawned on me that I fell asleep without taking it out of my book bag. I yawn and stretch as I get up to walk over near the window to retrieve my backpack. When I lift my head and glance out the window, to my surprise, I see Daniel coming up the road on his tiny red scooter. *What is he doing here so early,* I think. *Okay, get it together, Naomi.* I dash over to my dresser to get a fresh pair of jeans and a t-shirt. *Just because he is here doesn't mean you have to say anything about anything. Joseph is just a guy you met and you are not obligated to tell him everything.* All of a sudden the doorbell rings. I hear my mom's footsteps and then Daniel's voice. *I will break the news about our breakup later,* I think. I tame my frizzy, sleep-mangled hair. I turn around and just like that, there he is standing in my door way, smiling from ear to ear.

"I am so happy to see you, baby. What happened to you yesterday? I called your cell phone several times but I never got an answer. Then I called the house, but all I could get was a busy signal."

Wow, he has no idea how much has changed since yesterday. Everything is different now and I feel a sudden sadness for him because he is so clueless to the fact that I have been thinking about breaking up with him the entire time he has been worrying about *me*.

"Oh, my mom sometimes takes the phone off the hook because we have had several bill collectors calling lately," dodging his first question until I can think of a reason for not answering my cell phone.

"Oh, well why didn't you answer your phone?" At this point his questioning begins to sound like demands. He walks over to my bed and sits down without asking permission.

With sarcasm and a sigh, I reply, "Well just have a seat, Daniel." I roll my eyes at his lack of respect and continue with my alibi, "I had a rough day yesterday. Ms. Rayburn asked me to stay after class because she caught me daydreaming again."

"Yeah, I didn't see you after her class. Did she send you to the office or something?"

"No, I left after that."

Surprised at the news he retorts, "You left where—the school!?"

"Yeah, I just took a walk."

"Wow, Naomi. You surprise me more and more every day."

Then he approaches me with outstretched arms to hold me. I walk hesitantly toward him, thanking God that I told the truth and still managed to keep Joseph a secret. As he holds me he talks about how he missed me and how much he is glad I'm okay. This only makes me feel even worse. He tries to pull back a bit to look at me and I know this is his usual body language when he wants to kiss me, so I continue to lay my head on his shoulder, unmovable.

"Hey, look at me." I follow his orders and there we are face to face. For a few moments he searches my eyes and asks, "Is everything okay babe?" It's hard to look him in the eyes with everything that is going on in my head, so I drop my head and break away to walk over to my window. He follows me and takes a position right behind me. *Okay, Naomi, don't chicken out, this is your chance.*

"You don't look so well, babe. Are you okay?"

"No." I say with a raspy voice. I look at him once more, at his familiar gray eyes. I feel horrible for leading him on all this time, giving him more time to fall more and more in love with me while I'm at a stand-still trying to find the perfect time to break it off with him. That perfect time never comes, because I have developed some type of strange attachment to him. He is my comfort. He is all I know; my first love, my first kiss, the first male in my life since my dad left.

"Well tell me maybe I can help. Do you need me to pick you up some medicine from the drugstore?"

Great, he thinks I'm not feeling well. This buys me more time to come up with the right words to tell him how I feel.

"No, I have some meds to get me through the day. Besides I think I might be coming down with the stomach flu."

"Aw, baby, I'm going to stay with you all day to take care of you," he says as he pulls me close to him and kisses me on my shoulder.

At that moment I am reminded of Joseph's invitation to the library this afternoon. "No, babe, you can't stay; I don't want to pass my germs on to you. This can be contagious." He releases me from his embrace and moves away slowly.

"Yeah, you're right. I can't get sick *now*; I have a wrestling tournament on Monday."

41

I turn to face him, no longer scared and timid, "Oh yeah," I say. "I forgot about that. Have you been practicing lately? I don't remember hearing you say anything about practicing."

With a cocky smile, "Babe, please, you know better than anybody that I don't need to practice."

"Okay Mr. Cocky, don't come whining to me on Monday if you get too tired during the second match. You know you have to build your stamina before tournaments of this magnitude. This is the finals, Daniel."

"Alright, babe, if it means that much to you, I will try to get some practicing in today, since you are temporarily out of service." He says this as he approaches me with one of his sneaky smiles. He locks his arms around my waist and stares into my eyes.

"I love you, Naomi. You always bring out the best in me." Then he leans in for a kiss.

"No, Daniel," I say as I break away from his hold, "I told you, I may be contagious."

"That you may, my dear," he responds, and then he laughs and gives me a light tap on my butt.

I shoot him a stern glare, "I've told you not to do that, Daniel."

With his hands in the air, like I had just told him to freeze, he grins and backs up to the doorway, "Okay, okay, I'm sorry. I'll call you this evening?"

"Sure, Daniel."

"I love you, Naomi" he yells as he walks down the stairs.

"Yeah, me too," I say under my breath.

"I heard that," he yells back up to me.

꒰ꓸ

It takes me three whole hours to find something to wear. I don't want to wear anything tomboyish, and I really don't want to wear something too over the top. I finally decide on a pair of blue jeans that fit just right and a red, slim fitting, crew neck t-shirt.

During my attempt to tackle my bee hive of hard-to-manage curls, I realize I have only fifteen minutes to finish or I will be late. As I pull together my usual high ponytail, my hands begin to shake. Why am I so nervous about meeting him? Maybe it's because yesterday I met him by chance and today I am actually making a conscious decision to meet up with him. Or, maybe it's because I told Daniel a little white lie to keep him away for a day, so I could see Joseph again. I know that "little white lies" are not little at all. Sometimes the lies you think that are "little" turn into your worst nightmare. A lie is a lie. So, along with the butterflies, I have a large dose of guilt. I put on the last few touches of accessories: clear lip gloss and earrings. Then I examine myself from head to toe in the body size mirror that hangs on the back of my closet door. *Hmm, this will do*, I think. Then I grab my backpack and head down stairs. My mom is sitting at the breakfast table reading the newspaper, drinking coffee. I settle within myself to make our conversation short because I only have five minutes to spare.

"I made a whole pot of coffee, Naomi, help yourself."

"No thanks, I'm fine, Mom."

I proceed to the refrigerator to get a bottle of water. Drinking coffee with a stomach full of butterflies is not a good idea, especially not for me. My stomach is rumbling too much as it is and I don't want to have the runs as soon as I get there. My stomach rumbles right at the onset of the thought. When my mom hears my stomach, she puts the newspaper down on the table and turns slowly around to look at me.

"Are you okay, Naomi? It sounds like you have an upset stomach."

I close the refrigerator and place the bottle of water in the side pocket of my book bag. "Yeah, but I am fine. Just a little nervous, that's all." I never could lie to my mom or keep anything from her. She deserves to know everything that is going on with me, but using wisdom on what to share and at what time is key.

"Well, I am going to the library to meet someone I met yesterday."

With her eyes stretched open wide she says, "Oh, okay." She turns back around nonchalantly and picks up her newspaper again, pretending to read. Then she continues her questioning. I lean up against the counter with my arms folded across my chest, open to all of her questions.

"So, is this someone a guy or a girl?"

"A guy," I pull myself up on the counter to sit and make myself a little more comfortable. "His name is Joseph. We sat and talked for a while yesterday about the story of Joseph and..." I hesitate, "about a dream I had."

My mom turns around again with the same wide eyed expression.

"Really Naomi," she says with fear and tension in her voice. "When did you start talking to strangers about personal things? You don't know this guy—if he's a predator, a pervert, a serial killer!"

"Mom, he's not any of those things. I think I would have figured that out after almost an hour of talking to him. I mean, not many serial killers go around listening to bible stories and interpreting dreams."

She exhales, stands to her feet and walks over to face me. "Naomi, I know I haven't been such a great person to talk to lately, but honey, you have to be a little more careful. Are you sure this is a wise thing to do, going to meet a stranger by yourself?"

I turn my head to look out the window. I didn't realize how beautiful the day was until now. The sun is shining bright and there isn't a cloud in the sky. All of a sudden a memory of last night's dream comes flooding into my head. I remember the safety I felt, the contentment and the joy. I slide down off the counter, put my hands on her shoulders, smile and kiss her on the cheek. "Yes ma'am, I'm sure."

She squints her eyes and looks me straight in my eyes, just like she always does. She does this when she is searching for some hidden answer. My mom has learned to trust me, considering that I have basically been taking care of myself *and* her for the past six years. Deep down she knows I wouldn't do anything crazy and that I tend to make responsible decisions.

She waits a moment, walks back over to the table, and takes her original seat and finally says, "Okay." She gestures to the door with her hand, as she reaches for her coffee. "Go on and meet your friend, I trust you," and she slowly takes a sip of her coffee, and then says, "Oh, I forgot to ask, does Daniel know you are meeting this, 'new friend?'"

My mom is good about being very sarcastic after she has given you the supposed opportunity to make your own decision.

"No, and I don't think I need to tell him. I am not married to anyone, so I feel that I can be friends with whoever I please."

I walk over to hug my mom goodbye and head for the door.

"Make sure you are home for dinner, Naomi. I am making your favorite!"

Opening the front door, I shout back, "I will," and then I leave.

Chapter 6

This time I caught the local bus to the library because it was way too risky to walk five miles in the hot April sun. The streets are busy and crowded with vendors, passersby and bumper to bumper traffic. Saturdays in downtown Augusta are busier than normal and people are everywhere: sitting outside having lunch in front of restaurants, listening to live jazz or soft rock music, and some just browsing art galleries and souvenir shops. I walk one block through the throngs of people before I reach the library. When I enter the doors I am relieved to feel a cool breeze greet me. I say hi to the usual Saturday crew and head back to my already occupied couch and stool. Joseph is already here, sitting there looking even more handsome than I remembered. He is wearing a pair of black cargo shorts, and surprisingly a red crew neck t-shirt. I scan down to his feet and he has on a pair of black flip flops, and all I can do is imagine him on one of those commercials where all the guys are gorgeous and the wind is blowing through their hair. A smile cascades across my face and suddenly he looks up and answers my smile with one of his own. He stands to his feet and puts his thumbs into his front pockets, looking like heaven on earth.

"Well, I guess you're in a good mood today, huh," he says with a chuckle. "You showed up!"

"Why, what do you mean?" I shoot him a confused look as he gestures for me to take a seat next to him. I decide on sitting in the love seat adjacent to the blue couch he is sitting in. A confused look appears on his face because of my chosen seat, so he slowly sits down.

"Yesterday you told me your mood would determine if you came or not; I guess you're in a good mood."

I smirk, "I guess so, Mr. Telepathic Memory." I sit quietly for a few agonizing minutes, trying to ignore the fact that he is intensely staring at me, so finally I say, "Can you please stop doing that? You are really making me regret this."

"I apologize, it's just…"

I finally look over at him and he's looking down at the floor grinning. "It's just what?"

He looks up and clears his throat, "Well, I have never been at a loss for words like I am today. I don't know what to say, how about you?"

Wow, I think. I never met a boy, or man rather, that says exactly what's on his mind. Maybe it's because he's much more mature. *Lord please forgive me*, I think. "I'm fine, just thinking about the books I need to pick up before I leave." I lie and it tastes bitter coming out, but I stick with my story. Naively, I think, *I don't need him thinking I'm into him this soon. It's best to play hard to get, keep my cards and play them one by one, so I don't get hurt.*

Joseph grins again and runs his fingers through his wavy head of hair. "Man, you're tough." He grumbles under his breath, "I guess I have a lot of work to do."

I hear him clearly, but I pretend I don't. Leaning forward I reply, "Huh? What was that?"

"Nothing," he says innocently. "So, what books do you need to pick up, maybe I can help you find them?"

I reach in my book bag and pull out a notebook where I have some titles written down. "Well, my friend Emmy and I like to read novels together; well, not together, but at the same time, so we can discuss them. We have our own little book club, sort of. We barely see each other now, so this is kind of the only thing that is keeping us close."

"Sounds like a good way to stay close. Why, may I ask, are you two not seeing each other?"

I cut my eyes at him and say, "I get the feeling you already know the answer to this question—don't you?"

His expression is hard, "It's him, isn't it?"

"Yeah, they really don't get along so I try to spend my time with them separately, but most of my time is spent with him. He is pret—ty needy at times. Emmy can't stand him, and when they are near each other you would think they are an old married couple."

With the same hard expression he asks, "Did you break up with him yet?"

Double wow, this man is really straight-forward. "No, not yet; it's only been one day, Joseph. I can't break up with someone that I have been with for two years with only one day to think about it. Don't you think that would be kind of harsh?"

My heart flutters when I finally meet his gaze and marvel at his brilliant green eyes. It's getting harder to be sharp with him, but in some strange way, I love this hard expression of his. It seems so serious and authoritative, as he sits there, elbows on his knees with his hands woven together and squared shoulders.

"Well, from what you told me yesterday, you have been thinking about breaking this off for some time and, come on, Naomi, it's not like you're married to him."

I sit back in the couch for the first time, surprised and wide eyed, as if someone just slapped me in the face. I'm speechless, not because he's wrong, but because he said it.

"This bluntness is going to take some getting used to," I say.

Joseph finally sits back as well, runs his hands over his face and exhales into them. "I apologize, Naomi. I shouldn't have said that. I mean this is really none of my business. I just...," he leans forward again and takes his original position. Then he says it, "I just want the best for you." He looks me square in the eyes and I melt. He is being so brutally honest I don't think I can ever manage to lie to him ever again. I don't know how to counter his response, so I get up, notebook in hand.

"Okay, are you gonna help me or what?"

He smiles and rises to his feet, "Sure, it would be my pleasure."

The first book we look for is a romantic novel called, *Tears*. Joseph finds it quickly and we move on to the next book, which is a reference book that I need to write a research paper. This book isn't so easy to find, so we spend about thirty minutes looking in the wrong area only to find out from a help desk clerk that it is in one of the most unusual spots: in the nonfiction section instead of the reference section. He directs us to two large bookshelves where he suspects we will find the book. Joseph and I playfully argue over which bookshelf it is on and finally decide to agree to disagree.

"Okay," he says, "you look on the bookshelf you think it's on and I am going to look on the other one. If I find it, you have to promise to go to dinner with me tomorrow night."

The persistent butterflies that are stubbornly dwelling in my stomach do a dance. I smile and say, "Deal."

I head in the direction of my chosen book shelf. As I walk I realize how much fun I have had being with Joseph; no arguing, no pressure and most of all, honesty. When I get to the bookshelf my stomach jolts when I hear, "Naomi!" Not because Joseph has found the book and he's running to show it off to me, but because the voice that calls my name isn't Joseph's, it is Daniel's.

I turn around slowly when the voice is closer. I can hear my heart beating and I can feel its rhythm throughout my entire body. My stomach does a somersault when I see his face. Daniel is standing there looking at me as if he has seen a ghost. He looks as if he has been running because his hair is in an icicle pattern around his forehead from the perspiration, and his face is flushed with red blotches. I gather that he rode his scooter here and seeing that it doesn't pick up much speed he suffered the long, humid, three mile ride here.

As soon as I turn around he says, with a breathy voice, "What are you doing here? You're supposed to be at home in bed."

As all so called little white lies go, you never can stop with just one, because one little lie needs another lie to go along with it, so you don't get caught. Oh how I wish I would have just told him the truth. I wish I would have told him that I didn't feel like seeing him today that I wanted to go to the library to meet a friend. Now I'm stuck trying to figure out how to get out of this awful lie I told. I manage to conjure up a response that I think will get me out of this mess.

"Well, I started feeling a little better and thought some fresh air would be nice."

Just then I remember that I am here with Joseph and he could be walking up any minute now. I look over Daniel's shoulder and realize Joseph is nowhere to be found. The aisle of bookshelves across from us is completely empty. Daniel notices my quick glance and looks over his shoulder.

"Are you okay, Naomi? I mean, do you really think you should be out in public? How did you get here anyway—please don't tell me you walked?"

"No, I caught the bus." I respond with a meek voice, trying to seem physically defeated.

On the inside I'm feeling triumphant because of the fact that Daniel believes every word I say.

I have managed to get out of explaining my sudden appearance at the library.

Before he can ask me another question, I counter with my own, pretending to continue looking for books, I ask, "So what are you doing here, aren't you supposed to be practicing for your tournament?"

He grimaces, "Timothy wasn't home, so I didn't have anyone to run through the matches with."

"So what are you going to do? You can't just sit here all day reading *The Spark*. You need to get some practice in."

He smiles and folds his arms across his chest, "I guess I'm gonna have to wing it and spend the rest of my day with you."

Just as he says this, I catch a glimpse of red in my peripheral vision. I look over Daniel's shoulder once more, and there he is walking towards us, smiling, with that beautiful expression that I have come to enjoy. My heart stops, and I hold my breath because I know everything is about to come shattering down in this glass house.

"I'm sorry it took me so long ma'am, but I found the book you were looking for."

He hands me the book and I catch on when he winks at me and continues to smile as though we just met.

"Thank you Joseph. Daniel, this is Joseph, he has been helping me find the books I need to pick up."

Daniel turns around holds out his hand, "It was nice of you to help my girl."

Joseph just nods his head, as he continues to smile and stare intently, "No problem, it was my pleasure. I will see you later, Naomi."

He winks once more as he says this, then turns around and walks away. Daniel watches him as he walks away and continues until he turns the corner.

"What was the wink all about and how does he know your name?"

This is something I'm used to. Daniel doesn't like for me to talk to any males other than him and my math teacher, Mr. Frazier. Whenever we are together and there is an opportunity to speak to the opposite sex he assumes that responsibility and insists that I allow him to. This is another issue that I don't see myself being able to deal with. Jealousy and control are two parts of Daniel that always tend to get the best of him and keep us from getting further in our relationship.

Rolling my eyes I say, "Daniel, he has been helping me for the past hour, so we did happen to exchange names."

"There wasn't any exchanging of anything else, was there?"

"No, Daniel. Now can you please just take me home, I'm actually starting to feel sick again."

As we walk up to the checkout line, I do a quick glance around the library, checking to see if I see Joseph anywhere. He must have eavesdropped on my conversation with Daniel before he walked up because that was so sweet of him to keep our secret. At the counter, Daniel is mindlessly chatting with the circulation desk clerk and I hear the door open. I look up and there he is with his attractive smile holding the door open with one hand and the other hand he has up to his face. His thumb is up to his ear and his pinky to his mouth. At first I can't make out what he is gesturing, then it hits me, *he wants me to call him.* Then just like that, he's gone. I am stuck in time, wishing I could have spent more time with him, or maybe even asked him for his number.

༣

During the ride home I wonder why Joseph would tell me to call him if he knows I don't have his number. *Maybe he wants me to look it up in the phone book,* I think. But I don't know his last name, he never told me. In the mist of my thoughts, I become even more frustrated because not only am I on the only thing slower than walking--- a 15 mile per hour scooter---but it is so hot and humid that our bodies are sticking together. Now I really feel sick. We finally arrive at my house and Daniel takes one look at my sweat drenched face and he doesn't attempt to come in. He kisses me on the cheek and says, "I'll check on you tomorrow?" I am in the process of taking off my helmet when I become overwhelmed with a feeling of pity for Daniel. I have been lying to him all day; he only has been trying to help me, and all he wants to do is spend a little time with me. "Sure, that sounds good." Then I kiss him on the lips for the first time today. He holds my face with both hands and embraces it for as long as he can, as if it was our first kiss. I don't rush him, but he finally pulls away slowly, still holding on to my face he says, "I love you."

And I whisper back, "I love you too."

When I open the door, my mom is sitting on the couch in her usual spot. She looks over at me and informs me my dinner is in the microwave. I realize that she has no idea that I am supposedly sick with the stomach flu.

"Okay mom, thank you. I have to wash up first."

I go upstairs still thinking about Daniel, his sad eyes and the familiarity I have with him. I start to unload my book bag to make sure my books didn't get mixed up with Daniel's, and then all of a sudden Joseph comes flooding back into my thoughts. I pull out the book we found together and think of our conversations and all the fun we had on our scavenger hunt. Then I pull out the book he found for me. I giggle a little thinking about how he was right and I was wrong on the whereabouts of this particular book. As I am sitting there, I remember his gesture. Then it dawns on me; I open the front flap of the book and there's a note. It reads:

Naomi, I am sorry our day was cut short. Call me when you get some time to yourself.

(706)985-4444. By the way, I was right and you were wrong. What time is dinner tomorrow???

Chapter 7

Sleeping was no easy task, after all that had gone on today. I stayed up until two o'clock in the morning going over every detail of my day. My thoughts are comprised of Daniel and how horrible I felt for lying to him, but mostly I thought of Joseph, how much I am enjoying getting to know him and how I love being around him. Sometime past two in the morning, I fall asleep. I remember staring at the clock, praying to God that I fall asleep soon. Next thing I know I am shaking my head as fast as I can to awake from a terrifying dream. It's not the usual horror scene that I have every once in a while, but it's just as petrifying. Panting for breath, I turn to glance and look at the time, it's five in the morning. I roll out of bed and stumble to the bathroom. My face is covered in sweat. I bend over to splash my face with water. My hands are shaking and all I can think about is the last vision I had before I finally woke up.

I am running as fast as I can, but it doesn't seem to be fast enough. My legs feel as though there are fifty pound weights attached to them. There has just been an earthquake in my postage-stamp-size of a town, which is inconceivable because it is unheard of in the south. I hear on the news that earthquakes are happening simultaneously in other states, as well.

There has been a power outage for several days. People are losing their minds because they were not prepared for something like this. Stores are out of food, gas stations have shut down and there is no water. In the midst of this, I see myself encouraging everyone else. I seem fine; clean clothing, no appetite, and in my right mind. More days go by and things only get worse.

The sky is a bright red, streaked with black lines of smoke and mountains are erupting with sulfuric lava all around me, which is odd because Georgia doesn't have any sulfuric mountains. People are running and screaming to get away, but it's no use, the horror is everywhere. People are running to get in their vehicles, but as soon as they start the car it explodes, sending debris in every direction, killing everyone that is within 100 feet of the explosion. I miraculously survive several explosions. I continue to run, trying to get to safety, but there is none. After what seems like hours of running and dodging explosions, I hear something that sounds like a thousand lightning bolts striking the earth all at once. The sound is ear splitting. I grab my ears and fall to the ground. The ground starts to shake and then I see it. The loud noise was the ground cracking right beneath me. The crack is only as thin as a needle, but it is easy to see and notice because beneath the surface, a bright orange glow is shining through. I attempt to touch it to see what is giving off this glow, but my fingers are singed from the steam rising from it. I jump to my feet and continue to run. The loud sound strikes again, I look back and the needle size crack is now a yard wide. People are falling into the earth, cars are falling, and the ground beneath me is sinking, yet, I continue to run. As I run, all I can think of is the people falling into the earth screaming for help. It's a sound indescribable. I continue on as the ground continues to descend beneath me. Now the crack that was so tiny is no more; the entire world below me is a pit of fire and sulfur. This pit seems to be six miles below the surface and everything that existed has been sucked into it, except me. Running as fast and as hard as I can, with what endurance I have left, I can still hear the screams. Each time I focus on the sound of pain and terror of those people, I become more and more fatigued. It's smoldering hot and I am literally breathless. Still, I run until all I have left to run on is what is in front of me, there's nowhere to go anymore. When I have run until there is no more ground and I start to fall into that bottomless pit, I wake up.

Trying to regain my sense of reality is no use. I can't seem to get those images and sounds out of my head. It usually doesn't take me long to come back to reality, but I stand in the bathroom for the better part of an hour before I feel enough at ease to record my dream in my journal. As I sit recalling every significant detail, I realize what the dream is really about. There aren't any hidden messages in this dream. There is nothing to figure out. It is straight forward. This dream is a vision of the end times and the tribulation period. This dream is a premonition of what is to come.

Chapter 8

After sitting up for the remainder of the night, I decide to use the number that Joseph left for me in the book. Hesitantly, I pick up my cell phone and dial the number. I glance over at the clock and it is 7:35a.m. Several thoughts race through my head: he may not be awake; it's way too early to call a grown man; he may be at work; I will wait until lunch time. I lay the phone down beside me and continue to ponder whether or not I should call. *Oh, how I would love to hear his voice right now.* I sit up on my bed and adjust myself against the backboard. And after more though, I finally decide to call. Nervous and breathless, I dial the number and wait to hear the ring-back tone before I put the phone to my ear. The phone rings once and immediately my palms start to sweat when I hear his voice.

"Hello," he says, causing my heart to skip a beat.

It takes me a moment to catch my breath and I respond with an echo of "hello."

"Well, I am so glad you called. It's nice to hear your voice first thing this morning. Are you okay?"

I am speechless. "I'm fine. I…," words fail me again. What do I say? *I want to go out with you tonight or I just wanted to talk to you. Any one of those would be too corny and forth-coming.* I am still trying to play hard to get, even though I just called the man at 7 o'clock in the morning.

"Naomi, are you still there?"

"I'm still here, Joseph. How are you this morning?"

"I am doing great right about now. How are you?"

"Doing fine," I reply, trying to stay as calm as possible and not let on to how nervous I am. "I found your note in the book, so I decided that I needed to keep my end of the deal."

I discern a grin on his face and he chuckles out, "Okay, now we are talking. What time should I pick you up?"

This brings goose bumps on my arms, along with a slight perspiration developing on my forehead. I have never been picked up by anyone but Daniel. What would my mom say and do? I contemplate a different alternative.

"How about I meet you, and it would have to be somewhere out of the city lines because I would hate to run into anyone unexpectedly again."

"That's understandable, but how are you going to get there, Naomi? I don't want you taking a bus all alone."

How sweet, I think to myself, but I realize that I would probably have to borrow Emmy's car.

"I will see if I can borrow Emmy's car, don't worry."

"Okay great! Are you a picky eater, because I know a great Chinese restaurant right outside of town? It's a nice quiet place, where we can talk with no interruptions."

"Sounds good. What time and where is this place?"

"I can text you the address and directions, and is six o'clock okay? I have a few things I need to get done at the office first."

"Sure"

"I will see you at six then."

"Okay, I will be there."

"Alright lovely, talk to you soon."

With butterflies tickling my stomach rapidly, I reply with only a quick, "Okay—bye," and hang up.

Wow, he called me lovely. I lie in the bed rethinking every word he said and playing in my mind how I think the evening will go. Then I envision my closet and every cute outfit I own. I have to dress nicer than I did yesterday and maybe something a little more grown-up. As I lie there consumed with thoughts of all things Joseph, my cellphone starts to sing a familiar tune. It's Daniel.

Chapter 9

I let the phone ring a little longer than I normally do, but I finally pick up. I feel horrible, dirty, and deceptive. *How am I supposed to keep up this lie with someone I care so much about? I am going to tell him,* I decide.

"Hey babe, I am sorry for calling you so early, but I just couldn't wait any longer. You feel any better?"

"Yeah, much better," I respond, still thinking about how I am going to tell him I have a date with some *other* guy tonight.

"So, what are your plans for today?"

Wow, he is making it too easy. "Actually, I would like for you to come by, I have something I want to talk to you about."

"Sure, I was hoping you would invite me over. I have been missing you so much it hurts."

Feeling more sinister, I respond, "Me too. What time can you be here?"

"I will be there in less than twenty minutes."

"Okay. Please don't be late. I have to get ready because Emmy is picking me up for church this morning—around ten o'clock. I only have a few minutes to chat."

"No problem. I am on my way, now."

꩜

I get dressed fairly quickly, because I never put any thought into how I dress around Daniel. We are so used to each other now that none of that matters anymore. I sit idle for the rest of the time, waiting on him, rehearsing everything I know I need to say. Some of the options I come up with are too cruel and it hurts just thinking about them. Telling him about Joseph is just out of the question. I come to a conclusion to express how unequal we are, how he is on a different path than I am and we are drifting apart. Then, I realize that this is the exact same explanation I have given him on several occasions, which never works. At the moment that I rule this option out, the doorbell rings. I hear my mom greet Daniel and then his footsteps, pounding up the stairs. Before I can sit up well on the bed he is prancing through the door and rushing over to embrace me. Oh, how he loves me. He holds me tightly to him for several minutes and I allow the embrace for as long as he holds it. The entire time, I feel like my heart is going to burst from the pain; pain from the recollection of Joseph and how much I have come to like him in the past few days. When he peals himself off of me, he looks me in my eyes and recites the words I used to long so much to hear—"I love you, Naomi." I return the gaze, but feelings of guilt flood my heart so badly that I can't bring those words up out of me. He looks into my eyes and seems to have found something unfavorable in them. He furrows his brow as if he has seen something he didn't want to see. His hands are still holding my back, in a half embrace.

"What is it?" he asks. "Is there something wrong?"

"Yeah, there is." I untangle myself from his embrace, straightening myself up into a sitting position.

"Did I do something?" he asks pitifully.

This is torture because he has done nothing wrong, but it is all a matter of disharmony. The dream of me saying goodbye to him comes to mind and I immediately begin to cry. He grabs me again.

"Aww, baby, don't cry. Please tell me what it is. Is it a dream you had last night?"

As I sob into his embrace, welcoming it, I start to chicken out of the confession.

I respond, "Yes."

"Tell me about it. Maybe it will help. Was it about me?"

"No."

I pause hoping for a brilliant idea to pop into my head. An idea that would make this all go away, to completely change the subject and ease my mind. After maybe thirty seconds, something comes to me. I realize that I did have a dream that stands out amongst my most recent dreams; a dream that Daniel would definitely be interested in.

"I had a very vivid dream last night, about the end of the world. The world was in chaos and it started here, in Georgia."

Daniel releases me and goes to his knees right in front of me. He stares me right in my eyes.

Frantically, he says, "Tell me about it. Give me all the details."

At that moment I realized that sharing this with him would be a huge mistake. Letting the current circumstances push me to tell him something so serious and detrimental is very rash. Daniel wants so badly for me to publish a dream in *The Spark,* and he has been waiting for this very dream to occur to talk me into it.

He comes even closer and grabs me by my shoulders, "Come on, Naomi, tell me—don't stop now."

"Never mind, Daniel. If I tell you I won't hear the end of it."

"Naomi, this isn't about you! You need to think of everyone else who needs to know." He places his hands gently on my face and focuses his eyes on mine, "This is serious and I think it's about time that you take it seriously."

"Oh please, Daniel. All you are concerned about is seeing my dream in that foolish magazine. I will not be held accountable for the whole world going into disarray because of one of my dreams. If you would listen to me long enough you would know that there is nothing anyone can do about the world ending, it's inevitable!

The only way to ensure you are saved from the chaos is to believe in your heart and confess that Jesus Christ is Lord."

He releases my face immediately, gets up from the floor and walks over to the window.

With rage in his voice and teeth clenched, he says, "I am so sick of this Jesus character."

"Well, Daniel, you know exactly what to do if you don't want to hear about him," I retort. "He is a major part of my life, so if you are going to be in it, get used to hearing about him on a regular basis. If you can't handle that, then we are definitely wasting our time."

Arms now folded across my chest, I gaze at the back of his head, hoping he would just leave. Then, an aspect of the dream comes back to me. Once again I can hear the screams, the fire, and all the people falling to their death.

I muster up the courage to say, "This dream is about what will happen to those who don't know Jesus. This dream is a warning to all those who do not have a relationship with Him. Daniel, this dream is a warning for you, to get your life together before this all takes place. Jesus is coming soon."

He finally turns around and gives me a sinister stare that sends shivers down my spine, "I am eighteen years old, Naomi, and I have yet to see or hear from this mystical...," he wiggles his fingers as if he is sprinkling magic, "person you speak of. How do you expect me to believe in this Jesus dude?"

I release my stance and take a few steps toward him, "Just believe in him, Daniel, that's all you have to do, just allow yourself to believe. It's a simple and gracious exchange. He gives you eternal life for a simple decision: to believe that He died for your sins and rose from the dead."

"Naomi!" My mom calls from down stairs. I stand for a few seconds staring at Daniel, hoping that what I just said penetrates his heart just a little, but he holds his evil gaze all the more.

"Yes, Mom," I yell.

"Come here for a moment, please!"

"Okay mom! I'm coming," I yell back. "I will be right back, don't go anywhere." I say, as I walk backwards to leave the room. Daniel moves to my bed and takes a seat.

"I'll be here," he says.

I return, ten minutes after I left the room. My mom needed me to read a letter she had received in the mail from an attorney's office. The letter was summoning her to a meeting about Aunt Destine's estate, which I thought was settled years ago. We were both confused about the technical terms that were used in the letter, but after reading it several times we gained an understanding. She must meet with the attorney this week and she wants me to accompany her. I know I have to be there so they don't try to pull one over on her or have her sign something that she shouldn't. My mom has never been a people person and since she has basically become a recluse in the past few years after Aunt Destine's death, it would be heartless of me not to attend the meeting. When I enter the room, I notice that Daniel is gathering his things. He quickly turns around as I close the door behind me and throws his book bag over his shoulder. He looks frazzled.

"Hey, you're leaving so soon. Usually it takes me hours to get you out the door," I say with a grin.

"Yeah, I just got a text that my mom needs me at home right away." He hurries to my bedroom door, not making any eye contact. Before he turns the knob he stops, never facing me and says, "I love you, Naomi."

With confusion I reply, "Yeah, I know."

He opens the door and in seconds I hear the front door slam.

Chapter 10

Borrowing Emmy's car was easier than I thought. She is a server at one of the busiest restaurants in town and Sundays are always her busiest nights. After pleading with her for about an hour, she agreed to let me borrow her car. Although I didn't tell her what for, as long as I pick her up on time, she was okay with me having the car tonight. With Joseph's and my dinner date being scheduled for six, I figured I would definitely make it to pick her up by twelve midnight.

The directions Joseph texted me were simple and I made it to the restaurant with all of my nerves still intact. Once there, I flipped the visor down to check my face. I fix a few stray hairs and check to see if my lip gloss still gives off a glossy shine. With it being so humid outside, I put my hair up in a tight bun, ensuring that I didn't end up with a frizzy mess by the end of the night. I feel confident with my chosen outfit: pin-striped ivory and taupe Capri-pants and a taupe colored, short sleeve top with a lace embroidered ivory cardigan underneath. I decided on a flat sandal with ivory and gold sea shells that decorate the sash across my foot. Not being much of an accessory person, I go with a simple pair of dangling sea shell earrings and a necklace to match. When I get out of the car and finally take a look at my surroundings, I realize how cozy and private the restaurant site really is. It sits cutely on a hill adjacent to a river that is lit by lights along the boardwalk. Not many cars are parked at the restaurant, but there are many cars parked along the river. I continued to take in my surroundings and notice people walking along the river: couples holding hands, children running, people walking their dogs. I feel illuminated inside, watching and listening to what now encompasses me. "Wow, you sure clean up nice," I hear a familiar voice say, from a short distance. I turn around to see Joseph walking towards me, presenting me with one of his billion dollar smiles. He has on a white v-neck shirt and khaki cargo shorts, with a pair of sandals. I am pleased to see that he didn't dress up too much either and we almost match. He stops right in front of me and continues to smile.

I laugh sheepishly and respond, "You don't look so bad yourself."

"Well, I wasn't sure how to dress. We got off the phone so quickly yesterday I didn't have time to ask."

"You did pretty good without my help," I reply. The warmness of my checks notify me that I am blushing, so I smile and turn away to act as if I am watching the river again. Joseph steps up beside me, close enough for me to feel his warmth.

"I love coming here," he says. "It's always nice to get away and come somewhere where nobody knows your name."

Without looking at him I say, "Thanks for choosing this place."

We stand there for a few more minutes, people watching, and then I feel his hand touch mine.

"Come on, I am starving."

The server seats us near a window that looks out over the river and we order right away. It's so strikingly beautiful it's hard to focus on anything else, let alone, Joseph. He finally demands my attention when he reaches across the table and glides his hand from my shoulder to my hand and gives it a firm, but caring grip. I shiver with the onset of the contact and think to myself, *if he touches me like that again I just might have heart failure.* I immediately make eye contact, of which, I was trying to avoid.

"What's on your mind, beautiful? You seem to be in deep thought."

I gently remove my hand from his. Resting my elbows on the table, I place both hands under my chin.

I respond, "I'm fine, just enjoying the view." I deflect the question and ask him a question of my own.

"How was your day? What is it that you do again?" I ask, leaning in just a bit more.

He straightens up and clears his throat. "I do investigation work for the government."

"Wow, Joseph. That's a pretty good gig for a, what, twenty-four year old?"

At that moment the waitress returns with our food. Joseph gives me a side smirk, only bearing half of his pearly white teeth. When she places my dish in front of me, my mouth begins to water. I had ordered something safe: chicken fried rice with egg drop soup on the side. Although this is something I am familiar with, it looks and smells different. The chicken fried rice, where I come from, looks a lot greasier and there definitely aren't four different colors radiating off of the plate. This rice had carrots, scallions, peas, corn and a hint of red vegetables that I can't think of a name for. I am so ready to dig in, but I decided to skip my silent prayer and wait to see if he would ask me to pray with him. The waitress places his dish in front of him and his food smells and looks even better. His dish consists of sweet and sour chicken on a bed of brown rice. This sweet and sour chicken comes sautéed in pineapple, green and red peppers, and a delightful looking sweet and sour sauce. *I will ask for a sample later*, I think. When the waitress gathers her tray and departs, Joseph, without asking, grabs both of my hands and prays.

"Father, thank you for this day; thank you for this company and seeing fit for us to meet. I don't take this for granted. Oh yeah, and God, bless this wonderful meal we are about to eat, in Jesus' name, Amen."

I open my eyes to see him staring at me and still holding on to my hands. I grin a little and gently remove my hands from his. Is this really happening, I ponder, as I dig into my bed of rice? I stare down at my plate thinking of how strange it was to just run into this *man* that's everything I have ever dreamed of. Then it dawns on me, *he is a man.* I am only *eighteen.* I take in a small spoon of rice and focus in on Joseph, thinking, what does this man want with a teenager? As I continue to stare, he is full of smiles spooning up his chicken and staring off to look at the view. He doesn't notice my curious stare, so I draw in his attention with the most direct question I could ask.

"What do you want with a teenager?"

His eyes shoot in my direction, with surprise and seriousness. I don't regret the question nor do I plan on accepting a vague answer. My Aunt Destine told me once, "If you want a clear and direct answer, ask a clear and direct question; this leaves no room for an ambiguous answer." At the time I didn't know what ambiguous meant, but when I found out, it all made sense. He finished chewing up his food, while I stared directly into his eyes. He smirks and shakes his head as he wipes his mouth with a nearby napkin.

"Well, I am waiting," I said.

"Girl, you sure know how to get someone's attention, don't you?"

I shift in my seat, put my spoon down and fold my arms over my chest. If this doesn't show him that I am serious about my question, I don't know what will. He straightens his face, no more smiling, but all seriousness.

"Naomi, I don't see it that way."

"What do you mean? I am eighteen and you're a grown man. I haven't thought of this until now."

I roll my eyes up in the air, thinking of how stupid I have been. I mean, I thought of it once two days ago, when we met, but I didn't fathom going on a date with him.

"It's okay Naomi." He says grabbing my hand again. "I don't see you as a teenager, I see you as my equal."

Snatching my hand away, "Well, I don't see it that way."

Silence encompasses our space, while Joseph and I stare each other right in the eyes. I break the stare off and pick my spoon back up. Joseph holds his position, as if he is waiting for me to say something else.

Finally he says, "I'll wait on you."

I put my spoon down and fold my arms again, "Wait for what, Joseph."

"For you to turn twenty—or thirty, or however old you think you need to be to...," he pauses.

I fidget in my seat, uncomfortable with the silence and in need of a clear answer. 'What *are* your intentions with me?' I think.

I break the long silence with a curt, "So—I am waiting."

Joseph reaches for my hand from across the table and without any reservations, I willingly place my hand in his.

He exhales, looks directly into my eyes, and says, "I will wait until you think you are ready."

"Ready for what?" I ask.

He smiles really big and says, "To be my companion—my good thing."

Chapter 11

After dinner and a rather deep conversation, Joseph and I decide to take a walk along the river. I check my watch and it's almost nine o'clock, which is good because Emmy doesn't get off for at least another three hours. My mom has so much trust in me that she never gave me a curfew, but I respect that I am still a teenager and need to be in the house at a reasonable time. Before leaving the house she yelled, "Tell Daniel I said hello!" This was her way of checking to see if I was going out with the mysterious friend I told her about yesterday. I did not reply and pretended I didn't hear her, but only said, "See you at eleven o'clock." Then, I walked out the door.

As we stroll, I find myself wanting to know more about this man who so eagerly wants to know all there is to know about me.

"So, Joseph, tell me more about what you do? I've always wanted to find out what kinds of things investigators investigate for the government. And please don't use technical terms because I won't have any idea what you are talking about."

He seems enthusiastic that I have asked and responds, "To tell you the truth, Naomi, I haven't been given a legitimate assignment yet. I have only been with the bureau six months. Since I am just a rookie, they send me on coffee and donut runs. Most of the time, I sit in the office going through cold cases, searching for unfound evidence."

"Wow, I always thought that coffee and donut business was a myth." I say with a chuckle and then another question comes to my mind. "So is the bureau you work for actually called the FBI?"

With a solemn tone he says, "Yeah, and I thought it would be more than just sitting around being someone's secretary."

"Don't worry, they will give you a real case soon, I mean you *are*, technically, still a rookie."

"Enough about me," he says as he captures my hand in his. At first I feel a little uncomfortable, considering our last conversation about our age difference, but I succumb to the affectionate gesture. He asks, "So, did you break it off with that Danny character, or whatever his name is?"

I steal a side glance of him, "NO! And his name is Daniel."

He grins, "Oh, excuse me. Well...why not? The sooner you make that decision the sooner your future can begin."

For some reason I couldn't help but think that his comment had something to do with him and me, but I ignore it and deflect the question.

I blurt out, "I had a horrible, yet, triumphant dream last night."

In an instant, Joseph stops walking. He steps in front of me and looks me right in my eyes. He is so close I can smell his cologne and I can see his pupils are dilated. He cups my face with both of his hands and pulls me so close that our lips meet. Softness, sincerity, and warmth are descriptors that come rushing to me all at once. It all happens so fast that I have no time to react and before I know it, it's over, and our faces are just slightly touching. My eyes are still closed, but I know he is still close because I can feel his nose touching mine. As I am relishing what I just felt, Joseph embraces me. At that moment I am spun back into a familiar memory, the memory of a dream I had with someone embracing me, and our bodies floating up into the clouds. I feel that safety right in this moment and all the emotions felt in that dream that night. When I come to the realization that this is now a reality, I gently work my way out of the embrace and begin walking again. Joseph catches up with me and silently walks beside me.

Eventually he grabs my hand again and says, "I'm sorry, Naomi, if I offended you. I mean, I hope I didn't offend you?"

He looks at me, questioningly to see if this whole abrupt action is something that I wanted.

I respond with a small voice, "No, Joseph. I am not offended."

I return his glance and we share a smile of endearment, "But you *did* say you would wait for me."

⸙

We walked for almost an hour after that, talking and getting to know each other on a different level. I realize how easy it is to talk to someone who is so in tune with their spirituality, and someone who doesn't argue with you about your beliefs because they are also his beliefs. Being here with Joseph makes me feel safe in so many ways. Now it's time for us to say our goodbyes. We return to our vehicles and Joseph walks me around to the driver's door and opens it for me.

He grabs both of my hands and takes a position right in front of me. "Well, Miss Naomi, I guess I will see you soon?"

Looking down at his hands embracing mine I say, "Of course."

Then, I look back up at him and without any reservations, I lean in and kiss him gently on his cheek.

Chapter 12

After Emmy drops me off at home, I notice my mom fast asleep on the couch. As usual, I pull her blanket over her and leave her there for the time being. She eventually gets up and goes to bed, once she realizes I am home. Climbing the stairs, I replay the beautiful night I had with Joseph. Shockwaves travel down my spine as I think of the kiss we shared. *The KISS! Oh my goodness, how am I going to tell Daniel this?* I'm not, I say out loud, he doesn't need to know. Once undressed and in my night clothes, I hear my phone buzz. I pick it up and notice that I have a text.

'HOPE YOU MADE IT HOME SAFELY. TEXT ME BACK WHEN YOU GET THIS.'

'I AM HOME. THANK YOU FOR AN AWESOME NIGHT.'

'THE PLEASURE WAS ALL MINE. SWEET DREAMS, NAOMI.'

I lie in bed thinking of all things Joseph. The day dreaming turns into dreaming and all night I have visions of him. In one dream we were getting married, in another we had children—a boy and a girl and in the final dream we were older, and attending our son's college graduation. I woke up at seven a.m. on the dot, cheerful, in a sense, that I didn't necessarily have to be at school until 9:50, which is when Ms. Rayburn's class starts. My first two periods were electives, which I didn't really need the credits for, but I do need to keep up with my attendance for those classes. Emmy basically has the same schedule as I do, but since she works late nights on Sundays, she doesn't really keep up with attending those classes. While brushing my teeth, it dawned on me that I should write the details of those dreams down. Maybe they don't mean what I think they mean, or maybe there was something there that I missed. Usually when I write them down I see things that I missed. I placed the toothbrush back in the little green cup on my sink and rinse my mouth out. Walking back into my room, I mindlessly reached for my ruby red journal that usually resides on my armoire, but when my hand fell flat on the wooden piece of furniture, I mindlessly slid my hand further to the rear of it. *It isn't here!* Trying to stay calm, I look in the crevasses beside my television and behind the armoire, still nothing. I ran downstairs and looked in the kitchen, the living room and my mom's room. Looking in my mom's room was a waste of time. My mom would never touch my journal because she knows how personal that item is to me. Once I searched every nook and cranny downstairs, I went back upstairs and turned my room upside-down. The last place I looked was my backpack, but I came up short once again. Tired and sweaty from the turmoil going on in my head, I crash on my bed. Lying flat on my back, looking up at the ceiling, I thought through every moment of the last time I had my journal. "Okay, Naomi, think!" I say out loud. *The last time I had the journal I wrote down the dream about the earthquakes. Then, I placed it right back in its normal spot—but it's not there!* All at once the thoughts of having lost something so precious to me takes over my emotions. *Father, please help me.* I closed my eyes. Then, after two to maybe three minutes pass, I get a clear image of Daniel's flustered face before he left my house in an unusual hurry yesterday. I see him and me arguing over my dream and at that moment I open my eyes, one hundred percent sure where my journal is. I pick up my phone to call Emmy.

Chapter 13

In ten minutes, Emmy is at my house beeping the horn like a maniac. I practically fly down the stairs and out the front door. As I approach the car, Emmy gets out and walks around to the passenger side door, mumbling under her breath. It's obvious she wants me to drive. My thoughts are racing: *what if this idiot has already submitted it; no one will believe it anyway; where is he; should I go to the school or to The Spark?* At this point Emmy reclines in her seat and turns toward me, on her side.

With her eyes closed she spouts, "So why am I here again?"

"Daniel took my journal, Emmy, and I have to get it back before he does something stupid."

"And where are we going?" she says in an annoyed voice.

"I am not sure. Sometimes he goes to first period, sometimes he doesn't."

"Okay, wake me up when this is over."

"Sure," I say curtly.

༉

As I enter town going ten miles over the speed limit, I glance over at the tall tower, where *The Spark* is produced and I notice Daniel's scooter parked right out front. Dazed, I look at the tower and I hear Ms. Rayburn's voice, "beware of the tower." *Well, how am I supposed to stay clear of it when this imbecile has taken my journal inside of it!* I banish the recollection of the warning, so angry that my hands begin to shake as I turn into a parking space. I make such a sharp turn that Emmy rocks into the door and the impact wakes her up. "That idiot got here as soon as it opened," I mumble to myself. I get out of the car, but before I shut the door I say to my—disgruntle—best friend, "I will be right back." With no hesitation, I sprint across the street, dodging two collisions. When I reach for the handle, I am so startled by what I see that I stop in my tracks. Daniel is walking toward the door. When he sees me he pauses and stares at me like he has seen a ghost. He looks to his right and to his left as if he is contemplating making a run for it. When I discern this, I immediately pull open the door and there, right in the lobby, we have a face off. Three feet away from him, I shout, "What are you doing, Daniel?" Passersby pause in mid-stride to see what the commotion is. With shame written all over his face, Daniel holds out his right hand. I look down and there it is—*my* journal. I walk up close enough to snatch it from his hands and tighten my jaw to ensure that all sorts of obscenities, that I so rightfully can voice right now, won't escape my mouth. I hold my peace, clutch the journal to my chest, and then turn around to leave, but as I am reaching to pull the door open, I feel a hand on my shoulder. I pull away to turn and give Daniel a mouth full, but when I turn around there *he* is, the man who has been haunting my dreams since I was a little girl. My heart stops as I glare at a six-foot tall man, with paper thin, silver hair, so thin you can see right through it. He is wearing a long khaki trench coat and his eyes pierce through me. My whole body begins to shake as he opens his mouth to speak.

"Ms. Peterson," he says with a voice that sounds as if someone is calling up from the pit of his belly. It's slow and melodic and every word makes me cringe. "I have read your premonition that you have so graciously submitted. Your contribution is well appreciated, and we here at *The Spark* look forward to seeing your writings in the next edition. Do you have anything to say for yourself? This young man," as he points a long bony tentacle at the creep in the corner, "has shared so many interesting things about you."

All I can do is stare into his sharp eyes, so auburn that they almost look red. I shudder at the recollection of his image in my dreams. I am at a loss for words and nothing comes out. I want to say, *this jerk did not have my permission to submit anything*, but it is as if someone has placed their hand over my mouth, and for this moment I feel totally restrained. He waits for me to respond, but nothing comes out. He gives me a vicious glare and with his ghastly, scratchy voice says, "I will be seeing you then, Ms. Peterson. Your dream should give the world something to think about." He shoots a sly smile in Daniel's direction, places a black fedora hat on his head and proceeds to leave the building.

I am still frozen in time as Daniel walks over to me and says breathlessly, "Do you know who that was, Naomi? Do you know who you just missed the opportunity to talk to?" My entire body tightens and I am released from the restraints that I felt wrapped around me. I push Daniel in the chest as hard as I can and proceed to the door. He still manages to blurt out, "It was the owner of *The Spark*, Naomi! The owner!"

I stop in mid stride and turn around. Walking slowly toward him I spout, "Yes, I know exactly who that was," I take more steps toward my so called best friend. "It was literally my worst nightmare, Daniel! Couldn't you see that, or are you as blind as I think you are?"

As I get closer, he walks backwards with his hands extended in front of him to block what he thinks might be another push.

"Naomi, I am sorry but don't you think you are being selfish? I mean if your dream really is a premonition of what's to come, shouldn't you warn us."

"No! God has been warning us for thousands of years! Read the Gospel of Matthew, Daniel, or Revelation!" At that moment everyone in the lobby stops to look at us and two men with black suits begin to approach me. I stop in mid-stride and realize how Daniel has made me step completely out of character. As they close in on me, I assure Daniel, "I will never trust you again. Stay away from me!" The two men reach me and ask me to please leave. With respect, I turn around and leave quietly.

Once out of the tower, I now stand on the sidewalk staring up at the sky. Everything in me wants to turn around, walk back into that building and rip Daniel's head off. As I stand there seeing red, I remember when I was a little girl, and being over at my Aunt Destine's house. She was in the kitchen making me some of her famous Ramen noodles. Although Ramen noodles aren't considered a healthy lunch choice now, back then, we lived by them. She would fix me a bowl of beef Ramen noodles and we would sit in her room eating them while we watched soap operas. I hated watching those shows, but I loved spending time with her, eating my delicious noodles and watching her act as if the soap opera actors really existed. She would yell at the television and even call up her friends and talk about these people like they were real. "Girl, she done left William for that low down doctor. You think they gonna get back together?" I would sit and laugh on the inside, hanging on every word she said. On this particular day, Aunt Destine had to switch over because someone was calling her on the other line. Listening intently, I realized she was talking to my mom. My mom was calling from work and from the looks of Aunt Destine's face, my mom must have been pretty upset. "Johanna calm down and tell me exactly what happened. Uh-huh, yeah—she what!? Stay put Johanna, don't you dare go back in there. I will be there in five minutes."

In seconds, Aunt Destine had on her shoes, she grabbed me by my arm and said, "Come on—girl we have to go get your mamma before she kills somebody." Once we got there I could see my mom sitting in her blue hatchback Honda. She had her head down and to my surprise she was laughing. "Oh Lord," my

Aunt Destine murmured, "I hope she hasn't done anything crazy." We pull up right beside the car. Aunt Destine throws open her door just as she puts the car in park. She almost flies to the driver side door of momma's car. "Open this door, Johanna," she shouts as she bangs on the window. Momma continues to grin looking down at something, something that must have been very funny because she doesn't look up at all. "Johanna," my Aunt Destine says in a more calm voice, "You know that she isn't worth it—you know that he isn't worth it. Look over there in that car. You see what you have to live for?" At that moment my mom looks over at me and stares right into my eyes. She begins to weep into her hands and when she lifts her hands to her face, I see what she was looking down at the entire time. It was a silver semi-automatic pistol with a wooden handle. I had seen this gun before; it was the same gun that momma would sleep with under her pillow when daddy didn't make it home at night. "Now, roll down the window, Jo. Come on, let's get out of here." Momma finally opens the door and gets out of the car. Aunt Destine embraces her and slowly removes the gun from her grasp. By this time, I am out of the car too, wondering what happened so horrible at work that momma had to bring that gun with her.

Momma whispers as tears roll down her face, "I am tired Des, I am so tired."

Aunt Destine responds, "I know, Johanna, I know. Sometimes we have to step back into ourselves and cast all the mess, all the heartache to God. That's the only way we are going to overcome and be victorious. Cast your care, Sis."

With that memory still resonant in my thoughts, I wait for the coming cars to pass and approach Emmy's car. When I go to open the door, I notice that Emmy is nowhere to be found. I look around and with defeat running through my body, I lean up against the car and stare down at my journal. I open up to where the bookmark still resides, in the same place where I made my last entry. I am astounded that my last entry has been ripped out. *He tore the page out,* I yell internally. I close the journal immediately, turn around, and hit the hood of the car. "Is everything okay?" I hear a familiar voice say, but I ignore it because I am so consumed with every type of emotion that I can't function to answer with a resounding NO! *Cast your care,* I hear Aunt Destine's voice say, but this is all too fresh in my mind: the betrayal, the lies, and the selfishness. The voice is closer now, "Naomi, are you okay?" Arms are now holding me and the tears begin to flow. I feel hands cupping my face, and they lift my face to his.

"Joseph," I say, before I feel the ground fall from my feet.

Chapter 14

In the darkness, I hear Emmy's voice, "Is she okay?" I hear cars, horns, and another voice that triggers tension to cascade down my spine. I tense up and feel the warm embrace that causes it to subside. "Shh, I think she's coming back to us," Joseph says. I open my eyes to see a throng of people surrounding me. Joseph is the first face I see, so I smile, then Emmy, two men in black suits—the same men who threw me out of Spark Towers—a few ladies, and *him*. When I lay eyes on him all I want to do is start crying all over again.

"Are you okay?" Joseph says.

In a very apologetic voice, Emmy whines, "I am sorry I left the car, Naomi. It was getting too hot in there."

I groan as I sit up on the ground, "I am fine. What happened?"

Joseph starts, "Well, you were over here beating up this poor car when you caught my attention, so I came over to see what was up. You started sobbing and then you just collapsed."

"It's my fault," Daniel sobs out. "I shouldn't have..." and he stops in mid-sentence.

"Yes, you are so right—you shouldn't have." I say from the corner of my mouth and shoot him a critical glare.

"He shouldn't have what?" Joseph asks.

"Joseph, can you take me home?"

"Sure, Naomi," he says as he picks me up off the ground, "but I don't know where you live."

"Wait a minute," Daniel says. "You know each other?"

"Yes." Joseph and I say simultaneously. As Joseph adjusts my limp body in his arms, Emmy and Daniel both look at us with shock.

I rest my head on Joseph's shoulder and mumble into his neck, "I will tell you how to get there." Joseph instructs Emmy to go on home, like he has known her for years. He ignores Daniel and attempts to walk away.

With a jealous rage consuming him, Daniel says, "Wait a minute," and jumps in front of Joseph to block his path.

Joseph says forcefully, "Wait for what? For you to make her so upset again that she passes out? I don't think so!"

I don't even make eye contact with the betrayer; I continue to lay my head on Joseph's firm shoulder, too weak to respond. Holding my journal close and tightly to my chest, I notice that there is no further response from Daniel. Joseph walks past him; I close my eyes, and lose myself in the darkness once again.

ᴣ

Laughter and casual conversation interrupt my dreams of running over Daniel with an eighteen wheeler. I wake up frustrated that I couldn't finish the dream, but I am confused as to how I got on my living room couch. I sit up slowly, feeling a little dizzy when I realize that I hear Joseph in *my* kitchen. I turn around to look to see if I am hallucinating, but to my surprise he is sitting down at *my* kitchen table talking to *my* mom. I turn back around to process all of this then, I get up and begin a slow stroll to the kitchen. As I get closer, I can see my mom is in good spirits and she doesn't seem the least bit angry that some strange man brought me home. Joseph is in the middle of telling her some story about a kid who manages to send his unit on a wild goose chase for his so-called missing mom. She is laughing so hard tears are filling her eyes. She stands to her feet because the bitter-sweet pain of the laughter won't allow her to contain herself in her chair. She leans over the sink to keep herself standing. I reach the thresh hold of the kitchen and Joseph notices me, but he continues to tell the story of how this little boy was a runaway who only wanted to spend the night in an FBI headquarters. I lock eyes with him, admiring how he has managed to win my mom over and also give her so much joy, which she has not had much of in the past few years. Finally, the story stops and my mom manages to get a grip of herself. She notices me and wipes the tears from her eyes.

"Hey, Naomi," she says breathlessly. She's out of breath so she stumbles over to her chair. "As you can see, I met the famous Joseph. I mean, I just found out his name, but this is the friend you went to meet the other day, right?"

I walk over to the table and pull out a chair. "Yes ma'am, this is him."

"Well, he is pretty funny. I never met an FBI agent before," she says raising one eye brow, which usually means, we have to talk about this later. She seems like she is in such a good mood. Her hair is down, and she has on fresh clothes, not that raggedy old bathrobe that I can't seem to get rid of. My mom actually looks happy today. Joseph gives off a shy grin and hangs his head.

"Ah, Mrs. Peterson, I told you I'm just a rookie. I haven't had a big case yet," he cuts his eye at her and says, "except for the case of the 'Runaway FBI Fanatic.'"

My mom bursts out laughing again and I still for the life of me can't figure out what is so funny about the story. She finally calms down and notices that Joseph and I haven't said one word to each other.

"Okay you two. I will get out of your hair, but when you get a chance, Miss. Secretive Peterson, we need to talk."

I glare over at her and ask, "About?"

With both hands on her hips and a roll of her neck, she spouts, "How about, 'Mr. FBI' bringing you home passed out?"

"Okay, we can talk about that as long as afterwards you can talk to me about why you are all dressed up."

She smirks, does one of those struts she used to do when she was flirting with my dad, over to the kitchen door and says, "Deal."

Joseph and I sit in silence for a few moments after my mom leaves. He sips on a cup of coffee, patiently, while I muster up the ability to tell him how my so called "boyfriend" submitted the most profound dream I have ever had to the most corrupt magazine in the country.

"So how did you get me home—seeing as how—I was passed out and you didn't know where I lived?"

He sits his cup down, "First of all, I have training on how to find people, and second, you were smart to put your address on the inside of your journal." He chuckles, "I just put the address in my GPS and here we are."

"Please tell me you didn't read anything else that is in my journal."

Joseph straightens his face, "Naomi, I would never betray your trust and do something like that."

"Well it's nice to hear that some people still respect other people's property." At that moment, I hear a melody coming from the kitchen counter. A familiar tone that makes me cringe. Joseph gets up from his seat to walk over to get it and I spat out, "Don't answer it!"

He stops in mid-stride, "I wasn't, and I was only going to get it for you." He picks it up to see who the caller is, "Oh, it's Danny boy."

I drop my face into both of my hands and say through my teeth to correct him, "It's Daniel."

Joseph sits back down as he silences the phone. I feel his warm hand touch my shoulder.

"So are you going to tell me what happened?"

With my face still covered with my hands I say, "It's a long story."

He moves his chair right beside mine. He places his arm around me and says, "All I have is time."

It takes a good thirty-five minutes, and a lot of tears to get through the entire story of how I ended up kissing the concrete in front of Spark Towers. Joseph sits back in his chair and folds his arms.

"Why didn't you tell me about this dream?"

"Well, I tried to—the night of our first date."

"And what stopped you?"

I can feel my face warming up again when I say, "A kiss."

Joseph blushes at this recollection, "Oh, right. I guess that must have completely made you forget." I push his arm off of me and we share a playful moment.

"So, back to business," Joseph straightens up in his chair and becomes this stoned-faced FBI agent. "We are going back to get your journal entry and explain to them that their acquisition of this document was fraudulent."

My eyes light up at the thought, but then I am perplexed at the vision I am encountered with; an image of that paper thin silver hair, that brown trench coat, and fedora hat, cause me to shut down.

"I can't, Joseph," I sob.

"Why not, Naomi? You have every right to. Although this is a very profound dream, it may not be one that should be shared with the world."

"It's not that, Joseph," I say with frustration, "It's the man we have to see in order to retrieve my journal entry."

"Well, who is he?"

"That's another long story in itself," I moan tiredly and plant my face in my hands once again.

Chapter 15

After telling Joseph all about the owner of *The Spark* and revealing to him the terrifying dream I have had since I was a little girl, he understood why I could never go back to that place. We both knew that this signified danger. Surprisingly, he also remembered the warning Ms. Rayburn gave me. Reflecting on what she said made me all the more leery to step a foot in that tower. We agreed to wait it out and see what happens. Maybe they wouldn't print it, since it was obviously stolen. He stayed for another hour and we talked about the dream: what it meant or what it was warning me of. He finally left around two in the afternoon and I decided to go and talk with my mom.

I check in the living room to see if she is in her normal spot, on the couch watching cowboy shows, but she isn't. I go upstairs only to find her in her bedroom, sitting on her bed. She's holding something in her hand, which I can't quite make out, and looking down at it. I push the door slowly, trying not to disturb her. She looks up at me and I can see that she has been crying.

"Mom, what's wrong?"

I go and take a seat right beside her. When I sit down, I can see what she has been looking at. It was a picture of her and Aunt Destine when they were younger. Momma looks around my age in the picture and Aunt Destine is even more shockingly beautiful in this photograph than she was during the time I'd seen her face to face. She looks exactly how I remember her only she is thinner and her hair is pulled up away from her face.

"I just miss her so much, Naomi, so very much," tears run down her cheeks and traces Aunt Destine's face with her finger, shaking her head.

"She is with us mom—cheering us on. I can sense her every day."

She quickly looks at me with tears running down her face, "You can? When? How?"

I tell her the whole story, about the dream, Daniel stealing my journal to submit my dream to *The Spark*, my memory of her sitting in the car holding the gun, and finally how I ended up in the arms of an FBI agent.

"You see, Mom that was Aunt Destine then, reminding me how anger and rage can only lead me into trouble. She may not be here physically, but she left us with so much of herself that her example can never fade. It doesn't matter that her body is no longer with us, her wisdom still remains. "

She exhales, "You know, you are right, kiddo. I guess I never thought of it that way." She smiles and puts her arm around me, "Do you know why I was sitting in the car that day holding that gun?"

"No, I have thought about it, but I never thought to ask. I knew that whatever it was it definitely would hurt you all over again if you had to discuss it."

She looks back down at the picture, "It was a month before your dad left us. I had been hearing rumors about him being with another woman, but as usual I would just ignore it. The night before, I had received a phone call from a strange woman. She had said, 'Your husband is sleeping here on my couch, you might want to come and pick him up.' I was dumb-founded and thought someone was playing a trick on me, so I just hung up in her face. A few minutes later, the phone rang again. The same number appeared on the caller-ID, but this time it was your dad. From the sound of his voice I knew he was drunk, so again that became my justification for him being at this woman's house. I didn't want to believe the obvious. He told me he would be coming home soon, but in the background I could hear *her* saying, 'No you are not, I will kill you and her if you leave.' You see this whole thing was just to let me know he was there, she didn't want me to pick him up; she wanted to end our marriage."

I am confused. I don't understand how this all led up to my mom being in that car that day holding a gun.

I asked, "What caused you to bring that gun to work, then?"

Without looking at me, she stared straight ahead at the wall, as if she was right back there in that car that day.

"Your dad did come home that night and before he did, I realized who that lady was that was calling my house. She was the same lady I work with who was spreading the rumors to my co-workers."

I interrupt, "What rumors?"

"Rumors I don't care to repeat, even after all these years." She continues the story without breaking her gaze from the wall. "I recognized her voice. When I realized this, I went to my room, got my gun, and put it in my glove compartment in my car."

"What did Dad say when he got home?"

"We argued but not enough that it would wake you. He admitted that he was having an affair with that lady, but I was in denial. I just wanted to keep our family together. I went to work the next day anticipating that she would get in my face, but she did something worse, something I never could imagine that any human being could do. She talked to all of my friends and all of her friends about your dad and things she should never have spoken of. She also told them about how he would help her and her son out financially. By the time the third co-worker came up to me to tell me about the new rumors, I was in a rage. I had to get out of there. That's how I ended up in the car. I knew if I didn't call Destine, I would do something that I couldn't take back."

"Wow," I said, shaking my head in disbelief.

I was so young and naïve that I never knew any of this was going on. I mean, I found out eventually that he cheated, but I didn't know my mom was going through all of *this*. She finally blinks out of the trance, gets up and walks over to her dresser. She begins putting on her pearl earrings as she reminds me of the events that took place after that day.

"If you can remember, Naomi, two days later is when I had that nervous breakdown. I had to let go of that job because my nerves where shot after that. Eventually, my doctor diagnosed me with high blood pressure. Two months later your dad left. I told him to leave even though, deep down, I didn't want him to." She turns to face me, "I didn't want you to grow up knowing that I accepted a man cheating on me."

I stand to my feet, looking her straight in the eyes, "But, Mom, you have been so unhappy without him," and the tears begin to flow. "I would rather have known that, than for you to live a miserable life without him."

She walks over to embrace me, tears flowing down her face as well, "No, baby girl, I am not miserable because he left. I was miserable because I felt that I let you, myself, and Destine down."

Right before I can respond, she squeezes a little tighter and says, "But, I am coming out of this pit I have been in—I now have something to look forward to." Still holding on to me she says, "Today, when I realized you weren't here to go with me to see your Aunt Destine's attorney, I went on my own."

She lets go of the embrace and walks back over to the dresser to put on her pearl necklace.

"Oh Mom, I'm so sorry. I was trying to stop that fool, Daniel, from submitting my journal entry."

"No, don't be sorry. I needed to go on my own. He gave me some good news, I mean *us* some good news," she turns around looking more beautiful than I have ever seen her look. "After six years of draw backs and confusion about your Aunt Destine's estate, they finally worked out all of the debts she owed." She walks over to me and grabs me by both of my shoulders and says, "Do you know that your Aunt Destine saved over a half million dollars in her lifetime?"

My stomach drops and I almost faint once again. I hunch over, out of breath, both hands gripping my knees.

My mom laughs as she rubs my back, "Yeah, baby girl, our struggling days are over! She left me a letter too. The lawyer said that she only wanted me to have it once I received the money and not before."

Still trying to catch my breath I pant out, "Why?"

"I'm not sure honey, but what I am sure about is that she had good reasons."

"What did the letter say?"

She goes over to her closet and pulls out some black pumps that I haven't seen her wear in at least a decade.

"I will let you read it later. We are going out for dinner. We both need a pick-me-up, but not the world's idea of a pick-me-up." She grins and slides her feet into the pumps. "Wow, they still fit," she says as she prances to the body length mirror that hangs on her closet door. "So, what are you going to do about this thief issue? Is Mr. FBI going to help you out?" She walks over to the doorway to turn off the lights.

"Yeah, I hope we can figure something out, or the world is in for a huge scare," I say as I follow her out the door.

She looks as if she is listening, but from the looks of her face and what I just said, she doesn't have a clue.

Chapter 16

Four weeks later

A s usual, the birds are chirping away outside my window, annoying me to the point of submission. I drag myself out of bed and fumble to the bathroom. *Come on, Naomi, it's your graduation day,* I tell myself. Although this week should have been memorable for me, I have dreaded waking up every morning. On Monday, the newest edition of *The Spark* hit the stands. And yes, my premonition was not only published in this horrendous magazine, but it was the cover story for the month of May. Front and center on the cover was a birds-eye-view of a desert landscape. The sky is cloudy with a strike of lightning hitting the earth, cracking the foundation. The headline read: ARE YOU READY?

After hearing about all of the legalities of retrieving my journal notes, I gave up on the pursuit and settled for it being published as anonymous. My mom was ready and willing to put up the money for the suit, but I didn't want Aunt Destine's hard earned money to go to waste, nor did I want Daniel to suffer through this either, even though I felt he deserved it. I was content with what they have, because since then, God has revealed much more about that dream. I was pleased to see that they published the dream just as I had written it: the occurrences of the three earthquakes, where they hit, and the chaos afterwards. Tuesday crept up, and it was the day that my mom announced that she would like to have a graduation party for me. This was completely unexpected, considering how much turmoil I had been in, which is why Joseph and Emmy conceded to the idea, insisting that it would cheer me up. Wednesday, although Joseph and I see each other almost everyday, we went on our second date—just to be safe. Trying to be discreet did work out as we planned because we ran into Daniel at a local diner. I was dressed causal but cute, and Joseph and I were just walking through the door, hand in hand, when we ran into Daniel as he was about to walk out. At first, a feeling of gratification began to fill me, but then the look he gave me shook me to the core. It was a look of despair, a look that you only see when someone you love has passed away. He stood motionless, for what seemed like an entire minute, staring at me, in my happiest state. "Hi," I said.

Without a reply, he pushed the restaurant door open gently and disappeared into the night. Although Joseph's and my relationship hasn't taken any huge changes other than a short hug when we leave each other and holding hands, the guilt of it all consumed me that day. I asked Joseph if we could take it slow for a while, which consisted of no more public appearances and less time talking on the phone. Half-heartedly, he agreed to these terms, but he is definitely holding up his part of the agreement.

Thursday was painful to endure. Emmy, my mom, and I spent the day together, arguing over décor for the party, the food and any other menial detail that I could care less about. All I could think about was Joseph, hoping he would call me, text me, or maybe even email me. It is painful to go through an entire day without speaking to him. Waking up this morning without a voicemail or a text is even more heart wrenching. Today is the day I close the book on my high school career, and I made up my mind last night that this is also the day I tell Joseph that I want to be with him, no matter who I hurt in the process. Today is the day I tell him how I feel about him. Daniel and I have been on the brink of breaking up since our relationship started and I am tired of letting guilt hold me back from making the obvious decision. It's a weird feeling to still have deep feelings for him, even though he betrayed me, but I do. I have feelings for both of them. My feelings for Joseph are fresh, emotions that are genuine and pure. On the other hand, my feelings for Daniel run deep. He is all I have ever known, my first love. Four weeks have passed since he betrayed my trust and we haven't talked since. It hurts so much, but I know I am making the right decision to tell Joseph how I feel about him. With everything in me, I know and believe that Joseph is my soul mate and nothing is going to stop me from expressing that to him anymore.

⁊

Sitting through graduation ceremonies has always been agonizing, but sitting through my own, with my best friend right in front of me, is something I will remember for the rest of my life. The speeches given are memorable, but now it is the time we have all been waiting for, for our names to be called and to close this chapter of our lives. With two-hundred and six graduates in my class, I notice that our royal purple gowns cover fifty percent of the ground floor. I look around and I see that the stadium is nearly filled with family and friends. When the person right in front of me is called, I glance to where I knew my mom would be sitting. I notice that Joseph has finally arrived. He takes a seat right next to my mother. In his hands is a large bouquet of white roses. His striking smile illuminates me from the inside out and I feel an overwhelming emotion fill my heart. *He came!* Everything in me wants to run to him, to hold him, and for him to hold me. I have missed him so much during that day I did not hear from him and the way I feel is enough to reassure me of what I need to tell him. Finally, I am in line anticipating the call of my name.

I inch closer as the three people in front of me are called. When I walk across the stage I can hear Emmy chant my name, a few cheers here and there from friends, and my mom and Joseph chant in a chorus, "We love you, Naomi!" In a faint whisper, a familiar voice says, "Well done, baby girl." Involuntarily tears fill my eyes and I reply, "I love you, Aunt Destine."

When Emmy and I say our final goodbyes to some friends and make our way to our favorite teachers, I hesitate to approach Ms. Rayburn, but I think, *what will it hurt.* As I approach, I notice she's talking to another graduate, but she turns around as if she knew I was coming. She had always been strange in that way: finishing your sentences, calling out the answer to your question as you approached her desk.

Smiling from ear to ear she says, "Miss Peterson," in her thick Jamaican accent.

"Hi Ms. Rayburn," I say timidly. "I just wanted to say goodbye, and thank you for the extra point that you so graciously gave me."

"Well, you earned it, Miss Peterson. I couldn't let my favorite student graduate from high school with a seventy-nine in chemistry, now could I?"

I knew this was kind on her part, but I also knew that she was trying to bring up something that I did not want to talk about, so I calmly said with a smile, "I appreciate it, Ms. Rayburn."

As I turn to walk away, I hear her excuse herself from her current conversation, and my legs seem to move a little faster than usual, but not fast enough. I suddenly feel a light touch on my shoulder and Ms. Rayburn call out my name in the eerie manner that she has since the beginning of the school year.

"Miss Peterson."

With dismay I stop in my tracks and slowly turn to face her, "Yes, Ms. Rayburn?" Her hair was in its usual state of disarray and she wears a black gown just like every other teacher, but hers looked less decent because it appeared to have been stuffed somewhere tight and pulled out in haste, never pressed or straightened out for such an occasion as this. She gives me a stern glare, cocks her head to the side, and I wait for a few moments, wondering what in the world she has to say to me.

Finally she asks, "Did you take heed to what I warned you about?"

Dropping my head, I respond somberly, "I tried, but some things were out of my control."

"I see," she says with a few nods, "I see."

At this point she seems to be thinking, but the anticipation is unbearable, "You see what?"

Immediately she looks up at me, as if I startled her, "You don't have control of what will happen during these hard times, Naomi, but what you do have control over is how you handle yourself and the people you surround yourself with. Don't be discouraged of what is to come, stick with what God has given you and love as though there is no tomorrow. You will be triumphant."

And just like a vapor she's gone.

ॐ

The car ride home was pleasantly silent. I decided to ride home with my mom because I knew Emmy would torture me with questions about Ms. Rayburn and my conversation. I never shared with my mom the strangeness of Ms. Rayburn, nor did she have any idea who she was. My distraction with what she told me prevented me from catching up with Joseph. He was gone before I could even lay eyes on him again, but my mom assured me that he would be at the party tonight. Once home, I run up to my bedroom to get a few more moments of silence, before all the chaos of the party begins. I flop down on my bed and suddenly I hear Ms. Rayburn's words again: *You don't have control of what will happen during these hard times, Naomi—Don't be discouraged of what is to come, stick with what God has given you and love as though there is no tomorrow.* I look over at my night stand, where now sits a sterling silver safe my mom bought me after the incident with my journal. She told me never to give the combination to anyone, not even her. I put the three-digit combo in, and turn the small shiny, silver nob. Once I retrieve my journal and open it up, I turn to where the page is missing. Staring down at the missing page evokes a feeling of dread and dismay on the inside of me. My stomach starts to churn and I feel as if I am going to be sick. It takes a minute for me to pin point what this feeling is, but then I figure it out. It's fear. It's that same feeling I get when something awful is about to happen, the same feeling I got the day Aunt Destine died. At this moment, I decide to write down the rest of the premonition, the rest of the dream that Daniel thought was so important for the world to know. When all the events of that horrible day unraveled, God revealed a portion of the dream I did not recollect at the time I recorded it in my journal. When I got home that evening, after having dinner with my mom, memories of accompanying dreams came back to me. As I begin to write these things down, I realize that writing this down is not such a good idea. It's too risky. Instead, I write Ms. Rayburn's words down. I place the journal back in the safe, turn the nob until I hear the click, and say a short prayer:

> *Father I don't know what's to come, but you know.*
> *You never sleep nor slumber. Help me to do your will*
> *and not my own. Show me the paths I should take*
> *and help me not to stray from them. Thank you for my*
> *safety and my loved ones safety. In Jesus' name, Amen.*

Chapter 17

It's now six p.m. and I can hear the guests arriving downstairs. It's obvious that Emmy has arrived because I can hear the music blasting as loud as it can go. As soon as I slip on my shoes I hear a knock at the door and then, within a second, Emmy is bursting through my door.

"Girl, what is taking you so long? Everyone is starting to show up." Emmy looks beautiful. She is wearing her favorite color, emerald green, which looks ravishing against her bright red hair. Her hair is curled tightly into coils that drape around her perfectly shaped round face. On Tuesday, we both picked out the dresses we would wear, and I knew that the dress she picked would look fabulous on her. Emmy has great taste, which is why I love going shopping with her. Her dress is strapless, but the corset style mid-drift is tightly drawn around her waist and it flows down to just above her knees. She picked out a crimson red dress for me, one that fits my taste perfectly. My dress has a sheer lace fabric that drapes the top of my shoulders. It fits just right up top, but loosens and shimmers as it flows down to my knees. I love how it modestly hides my curves.

"Wow, Naomi. You look like you are ready to wow the crowd," She says with a smile.

I blush, with only one person in mind and ask, "Is Joseph here yet?"

"No," she says as she walks over to sit down on my bed, "but Daniel is."

I stop in my tracks, "What! You mean to tell me that you and my mom let him in?"

"I'm sorry," she chirps out. Her face is now the color of my dress and as she is hanging her head she continues, "It's just that we arrived at the same time and he started going on about how he didn't mean to hurt you and how he was just trying to save the world and …"

As soon as I am about to start ranting at Emmy, my mom knocks and opens the door at the same time. I know at this moment I am beet red. I shoot my mom a harsh glare and I can tell Daniel has gotten to her, too.

I throw my hands up, "Mom, I don't want to hear it! You know I don't want to hear any explanation he may have. How could you allow him in our house, to *my*, party?!"

I fold my arms and flop down on the bed next to Emmy, who is still sulking with her head down. My mom walks over and kneels down in front of me. She looks strikingly beautiful; her hair is straightened in a gorgeous bob and she is wearing a beautiful floral colored dress. It's amazing how the absence of lack and worry can change a person's appearance and their demeanor.

She replies calmly, "Look, baby girl, you can't run from confronting him forever. Now, he has a good reason for coming here this evening. I suggest you hear him out."

"But Mom, I told you I don't want to see him," I retort.

At the tone of my voice she stands up and as she stands I lift up my head, knowing that my tone was completely out of line. She stands glaring at me now with a hard look on her face.

"Now you listen to me. I understand you are hurt, but you know good and well you are on the verge," and in a small whisper she says, "of falling for someone else. You can't open another door without closing the other! You need to talk to this boy. He has lost weight and to tell you the truth," she whispers again, "he looks like he is going crazy. I know you love him, and I know he loves you, but if you truly want to move on," she pauses and looks over at the door like he is going to walk in at any moment, "you have to give yourself closure and him as well. Take it from me—its horrible living in a messy chaotic house, especially when you continue to sweep all your trash under the rug. Eventually there's going to be too much under that rug and nothing else is going to fit."

I look at my mom with a half-smile because I know where this is going. She loves to use metaphors and analogies to explain her points, and sometimes she gets carried away.

She continues, with her hands now on her hips, "There's going to come a day when nothing else will fit under that rug because you have just swept more and more trash under it. Then, everybody is going to see the big mess you made and how you didn't bother to clean it up, *properly*."

"Okay, okay, I get it!" I say with frustration.

"Well, you asked for it," she says. "Now talk to the boy, tell him how you feel," she whispers again, "tell him you are finished!"

Then she gives me one of those priceless smiles and walks out. Within seconds, Daniel is at my bedroom door.

"Excuse me," Emmy says as she finally breaks her silence. She walks out of the room and she places her right hand on Daniel's shoulder, a friendly gesture that surprises me. He gives her a half-smile as she passes and just like that, we are within ten feet of each other.

Chapter 18

As I stand there gazing at Daniel, his golden straw-like hair, his short but strong stalky build, and his oh so familiar face, I am reminded of a dream. The exact dream I shared with Joseph the first time I met him. I remember a veil, angels that stood at least twelve feet tall and most of all, gaining the strength to tell Daniel goodbye. With the memory of that dream spilling through my head, I feel a fire growing within me, a desire, but also the courage and strength to finally say goodbye. Within a moments time I am ready to face the boy that I have grown to love so much, with the words I know he is anticipating. He shifts hesitantly, from one leg to the other, keeping his eyes fixated on the floor until finally I approach him, slowly and cautiously.

"Daniel," I say in a whisper.

He continues to look down at the floor with an expression full of shame, "Yes, Naomi."

"Can you please look at me?"

He looks up and there, in his electric pale-blue eyes, I can see the despair that my mom described. I can also see how his body has changed, his head now appearing to be a bit larger because of the tremendous amount of weight he has lost. *How can I hurt him anymore than I already have?* Then another part of me says, *how can you allow him to continue hurting you?* I settle within myself that this *is* the right thing to do.

"Wow," he says with a strained voice, "you look amazing."

I smile gently, "Thank you, Daniel."

Now that I am within three feet of him, I reach out my hand to him and he meets my hand with his. I guide him over to my bed to sit and I pull up the chair from my desk to sit down in.

We begin to speak simultaneously, "Naomi, I am so…"

And I say "So what…"

We both laugh and he says, "You go first."

Without any reservations, I take the liberty of speaking first. I gently reach for both of his hands and cup them in mine, and I look directly into his weary eyes.

"Daniel, I know that you are sorry for what you did, and I also know that you feel that what you were doing at the time was the right thing to do, but I really don't want to rehash the whole thing."

He looks at me with questioning eyes, but continues to listen.

"I don't want you to apologize anymore. I want you to know that I forgive you. Although, when I think of it, I do feel anger and hurt rise up within me, but nevertheless, I—FORGIVE—YOU."

At the sound of those three words I can see Daniels spirits begin to lift and he then reverses the grasp I had on his hands and now cups my hands with his. With his eyes eager to hear more of what I have to say, I continue.

"Daniel, you are all I have ever known when it comes to a companion. I have grown to love you so much because I have always felt safe with you, but for the past few months I haven't felt that way."

Daniel develops a crease on his forehead, and now his body has become tense as he sits, still gazing into my eyes.

"I know now that we have different paths we are traveling, and as you know my path is and always will be led by God."

At this point he cuts me off and with rage he jumps to his feet, as if the sound of that name incites rage.

He curtly say, "Is this because of that half breed that I saw you with?"

I stand to my feet, shaking from the inside out, surprised that he is having this reaction. I reply with a serious tone, "Daniel, now that is an awful thing to say! What about me, aren't I a 'half-breed,' whatever that is supposed to mean?"

He shouts back, "He doesn't love you like I do, Naomi! I need you, and I am not going to live without you!"

Feeling the sting of fear, I begin to back up toward the door, and to my dismay he is slowly getting closer. His face is red with rage and his hands are shaking. He continues to say, "I love you, I can't live without you." I continue backing away until there is nowhere else to go. My back is against the wall and the door is right next to me. *Open the door, Naomi, open the door.* I repeat to myself until he is now one inch away from my face, staring me right in the eyes. He looks me over, and asks, "Have you kissed him?"

I don't answer, I look away and he immediately grabs my face with his hands and turns my face back to his.

"I love you, girl," he says with gritted teeth and kisses me hard and forcefully.

I don't fight it, but I just let him. I let him, because I am scared and I know that this is how he gets when he is upset. The kiss continues for what seems like forever and my whole body wants to reject him, but I stick with it hoping that it will stop soon, hoping that this will calm him down enough to get him out of my house. Then, maybe, I can officially, call him and break this off forever, but the kiss continues and then leads to him pressing his body intensely up against mine. He then runs his hands down from my face, to my neck, then he continues touching me inappropriately. I open my eyes. I am now panicking. *What is he trying to do?* At this point I can't pretend anymore, and I tear my lips away from his and shout, "NO!" With all of my strength, I try to push him away, but it does no good. He continues holding me up against the wall, with his powerful, muscular body. I am helpless—defenseless against all of his weight and power. I continue to push and scream, although no one seems to hear. Then I realize how loud the music still is. Thoughts run through my head: *why did I agree to talk to him; why did I think that he would take this well; Lord, please send help for me?* At that moment, my whole world turns into a whirlwind. The door bursts open, I see faces: Joseph, Emmy, my mom, Daniel. I fall to the floor all of a sudden, hitting my head on something very hard and firm on the way down. I hear screams, I see blood, and then I feel the entire floor quaking beneath me. Everything is shaking and items from my dresser and bookshelf begin to crash to the floor. Dizziness overtakes me and everything begins to blur. My eyes start to close, but as I give in to the darkness, I see a haze of contorted bodies wrestling. I succumb to the slumber of blackness and just before I close my eyes, I feel someone hovering over me. A voice says, "You're okay, baby, I got you."

Chapter 19

A slow steady, BEEP—BEEP—BEEP, is what I hear consistently as I drift back down to awareness. I hear what seems like hundreds of voices around me, but I keep my eyes closed. One voice, which is deep and smooth, doesn't sound familiar. He is talking to my mom about me.

"She will be fine, a concussion tends to make you sleep longer because the brain needs time to heal."

My mom replies, "She's been sleep for over twenty-four hours, this is beginning to scare me."

Joseph's voice rings out amongst all of the commotion, but it sounds close, really close.

"Mrs. Peterson, I am sure she is okay. She stirred in her sleep a little last night and asked for water."

"I know, Joseph, she drank it, but she never opened her eyes," she replies, and directs another question to the doctor. "How come she won't open her eyes?" she says with a higher pitch in her voice.

"Okay, okay," I say, and open my eyes. "Are you happy now?"

I open my eyes to see a doctor standing to the right of me. His is a tall Hispanic man with dark features, but the most identifying characteristic is his thick mustache dripping down over his top lip. At the foot of my bed is my mom, with worry embellishing her beautiful face. At my left is Joseph, who is now caressing my face with both his hands, examining it for reality or make believe. He says softly, "You are awake."

My mom comes around to where the doctor is standing and the doctor looks at her. "Well, there you go, but my answer to your question would have been 'When she's ready,' and I guess she is ready." He smiles gently at her and she returns a gentle smile to him, then he leaves.

"He's kind of cute," I say with a giggle.

"Girl, hush. I can't believe you are playing around after scaring us like that," she practically yells, but gives in to a giggle, as well. She sits down on the bed to face me. Joseph finally sits up and retires from examining my face.

I ask, "What happened?"

My mom starts, "Well, your friend over here," and she winks one eye at me, "Beat up that lunatic you used to call 'boyfriend,' but I guess when we burst through the door you fell from his grasp and hit your head on the corner of your dresser."

Then Joseph chimes in, "As I was restraining 'the *lunatic*,' " he looks up at my mom and winks his eye, "an earthquake hit."

My mouth drops open and my heart begins to race. "What!" Suddenly I remember hearing the yells and what they were saying. I then hear the hundreds of voices again and see camera lights flashing. At this point reality really sets in and I realize that there are several news reporters standing outside my hospital room. I look at my mom and then over at Joseph.

He says, "Two other earthquakes hit simultaneously, one in Georgia, South Dakota, and one in California. Once it was over, word got out that there was a premonition about this. People wanted to know who had this vision."

With tears running down my face I ask, "Did anyone tell them?" I look over at my mom.

She looks at me endearingly, "Yes, but we are not sure who. That's why they are all here. The whole country is in an uproar and maybe the whole world. They want to know what's next, what we should do, what should we expect, and is the world coming to an end."

Looking at my mom's face I know that she wants answers too. I look over at Joseph and without me having to ask he says, "You don't have to say a word, Naomi. I will get you out of here." The essence of fear floods me as I lay silently. Eventually words come. I look up at Joseph, who is still giving me firm eye contact.

"I'm scared."

He replies, "God has not given us the spirit of fear, but of power, and of love," he paused and places both hands on each side of my head, and continues with the verse, "and a sound mind."

ᔓ

When night falls and after Joseph has run all the reporters away, he comes back in the room and sits in the chair next to my bed. My mom is asleep in the sofa at the foot of my bed. He leans forward and holds my hand. He gently brings it to his face and kisses it.

"What am I going to do? I don't know what to tell those people. I mean if I tell them the rest of the dream it would send everyone into chaos. I mean what if the last part is just a warning, what if it doesn't happen."

Joseph continues to kiss my hand gently. I appreciate his calm demeanor and ability to make every situation seem bearable.

"Naomi, everything is going to be fine. You just be sure to keep the rest of that dream to yourself. Don't even share it with your mom or me."

He finally stops kissing my hand and he sits on the side of my bed to face me. He leans down to kiss my nose. I gaze up into his sparkling green eyes and I am lost in them.

"I thought I lost you for a minute there, girl. I didn't know if that psycho had stabbed you or shot you. I just can't get the cry for help I heard coming from your room out of my head. All I can think about is you lying there unconscious and looking for blood or any wounds."

I just listen, trying to soak up every word that describes how much he cares about me. I feel this emotion rising in me. An emotion that sets my heart on fire, and it begins to beat faster than I have ever felt it beat. I place my hands on his face to hold it and then pull it closer to mine. He looks intensely down at me and I think I see pools of tears welling up, and before they can fall from his eyes *I* kiss *him* for the first time. His tears run down between our cheeks and my tears meet his.

After we have expressed our feelings for each other through a single kiss, he leans up, still staring down at me.

He says, "We have to get out of here tonight. The FBI wants to question you."

Surprisingly I say, "Why, I don't mind talking to them, I don't want them to think that I have anything to hide."

Joseph purses his lips and says sternly, "Naomi, you do have something to hide and when the FBI questions you, they want answers." He shakes his head and then looks out into the lobby of the hospital and repeats, "We have to get out of here tonight."

"What about my mom," I ask.

"We talked about it while you were sleeping. She knows and agrees that we have to leave the country—just for a little while, until this dies down."

I am in such shock that all of this has happened in less than two days. I know now that this is why I felt that sense of fear, this is what Ms. Rayburn was warning me about.

Joseph continues, "Your mom has purchased two tickets for us."

"To where?" I almost shout out.

"I can't tell you that now, but I will—soon."

After hearing that the FBI wanted to talk to me, it all seemed to be a horrible dream that I so desperately wanted to wake up from. Joseph mentioned to me that we would be leaving the hospital around midnight. My mom went home hours ago and now we have about an hour before we leave. While I am sitting on the edge of the hospital bed contemplating the events of the past week and this weekend, Joseph is pacing the floor, fumbling through his cell phone.

After watching him for quite some time, I finally ask, "What are you doing?"

"Trying to organize our flight schedule. We need to leave as soon as possible, but your mom and I were only capable of getting a flight for tomorrow."

Then I ask a question that I have been pondering all day, "So does the bureau know that we…," I hesitate with what to call our involvement so I just say, "know each other?"

He stops pacing and stares at me with a grin, "No, they don't know we are…involved."

I smile at the tone he speaks in and continue to ponder how all of this is going to play out. Joseph shared half of the plan with me, but he is obviously keeping a lot of the details away from me. I do know that we are leaving to go hide out at his apartment until it's time to catch the plane, but I don't know where we are going. I know that an FBI agent is supposed to show up tomorrow to take me to an interview, and I also know that Joseph is totally against me going in for that interview. Joseph continues to pace the floor and at this point I want some solid answers.

"Why is it that you are so against me going in to have this interview? It can't be that serious, right?"

Joseph stops in his tracks and with raised eyebrows he says, "No, Naomi, you don't get it. This country is in a state of emergency right now and you are caught right in the middle of it. Have you looked out the window or even paid attention to the news since you have been awake?"

I am puzzled, and the answer to his questions is, "*No*, I haven't."

He continues, "All three states where the earthquakes hit," he pauses and the look in his eyes scares me, "the damage was catastrophic; this country has never seen anything like this before."

He walks over to me and looks me in my eyes.

"I apologize if I am scaring you, Naomi."

I return his stare for just a moment then I get up and go over to the window, "No, I am fine Joseph. You are only telling me the facts."

I open the curtains, and for the first time, very vaguely, I see some of what Joseph is speaking of. Even at midnight the streets are busy, which is very unusual. I can see police officers directing traffic, a few power lines are still being repaired and workers are cleaning up debris from collapsed buildings. It's raining and I see hundreds of people flooding the streets on feet and in cars. Joseph comes up behind me.

He places his warm hands on my shoulders and I ask, "How is my house, does it look like this everywhere?"

"No, actually, your house is one of the few on your block that went undisturbed by the earthquake. What you are looking at is the worst of the results. Georgia didn't get it as bad as South Dakota and California."

As I stand there, all I can think of is the dream and how everything was being destroyed around me, yet I remained unharmed. Then, I notice the church across the street, which also remained intact. Joseph sighs behind me and embraces me lightly.

"I know that this is all horrible, Naomi, but just think, God chose you to reveal this to, an eighteen year old from a small town in Georgia."

I sigh too, and lean into his embrace. I continue to look at the effects of the earthquake and notice two identical black cars pulling up into the hospital parking lot. At that moment, I hear the church bell. Joseph whispers in my ear, "It's time."

Chapter 20

With everything that has happened, the hospital staff seemed to be so distracted with the news and the extra patients they have, they don't notice Joseph and me getting on the elevator. I am so nervous my palms are sweating. The elevator goes from the eleventh floor, to the tenth, the ninth, and every floor makes my heart skip a beat. When we reach the seventh floor the elevator stops and picks up two doctors who are having a conversation about a news report. They don't notice Joseph and me because they are so pre-occupied with the news of how the people are migrating toward the more centralized states and how the gas stations are hiking up their prices so high that people are literally stealing gas. The conversation sets off shock waves through my body, reminding me of the chaos that I saw in my dream. Finally the elevator dings when we reach the first floor and just as we are getting off, two men in four piece, black suits approach the elevator. One of them is tall and wide and the other is about Joseph's height, but he has the body of a body builder. Both men make eye contact with Joseph and Joseph stops in his tracks. His face turns bright red and I immediately know why.

"Hey Rook!" one of them yells out, "What are you doing here?" the other one says.

Josephs gives them a shy grin and gestures for me to back up behind him.

"Oh—well I was just checking on a friend of mine. She got hurt during the earthquake, but she should be checking out in the morning."

They both look at him and then at each other. It's obvious that they are puzzled. I make my way to a nearby bulletin board about five feet away from them, pretending to read a flyer that is stapled to it. Joseph is still feeding them the truth, but a very vague story, as the two, obviously experienced investigators, press him for a more detailed explanation. I listen intently and then I hear the deep smooth voice of Dr. Ward coming through the front door. *Oh darn, his shift starts at 12:30.*

"Hi, Joseph," he yells out, "you leaving so soon?"

I can hear the panic in Joseph's voice when he chokes out, "No, just—getting a snack."

"Wow," one of the guys spout out, "she must be a very close friend of yours if you are staying overnight?" and they both begin to laugh.

I think, *man, this is what he goes through every day.*

Just when I think we are about to get rid of them all, the doctor laughs too and says as he boards the elevator, "Well, I am sure Naomi is ready to get back home. Hey Naomi!" he yells out over Joseph's shoulder, "You need to take it easy; you shouldn't be out of bed yet. Get back in bed as soon as possible, you need some rest tonight."

Without thinking, I turn around and respond, "Yes Sir."

There's dead silence. The two men look at each other and then at Joseph.

"Did he just call her Naomi?"

They don't wait for an answer and the short stalky one reaches in his pocket and pulls out what looks like a photograph. They both examine it and then their eyes shoot across the room in my direction. "Well, well, well," they both say instantaneously. I then turn all the way around, to face them. Joseph hangs his head and presses his hands against his face in shame.

The two men, who now have names, agent Sylvester and agent Baynes, explain on the way to the Bureau, that they only need to ask me a few questions and then they will send me on my way. They make Joseph drive the tall agent's car, by himself, while I ride in the back seat of Baynes' car, with the both of them. As we ride to the office they laugh and make jokes about Joseph until I am at the point where I want to slap both of them.

"Could you two stop it?" I shout. "I am sick of hearing your stupid jokes! You're not funny!"

Agent Sylvester looks back at me and laughs out, "Oh, excuse me, I didn't know you and Rook were—that—close."

He bursts out laughing even louder and looks over at Baynes, who is driving and laughing even harder than he is.

"Wow, I can't believe they hired such immature, over-grown juveniles to be investigators for the government," I say spitefully.

Baynes looks back at me, "How old are you again?" he asked and then bursts out laughing again.

I shoot him a death stare and roll my eyes. Shortly after that comment the car falls silent and I meditate on what my answers will be, just how Joseph and I rehearsed before we left the hospital room.

꒰꒱

When we arrive at the FBI's secret location, I am surprised to see how far out we are from the city. The drive was just short of two hours so we are somewhere between Atlanta and Augusta. It's almost three in the morning, and it is so dark I don't recognize anything but murky shadows of trees surrounding us on every side. I look back to see if Joseph is still following us, and I can't tell because of the deep darkness. We get off on exit 147. We travel a couple of miles down a dark road with nothing but an abandoned gas station. As soon as we pass the gas station, Baynes makes a quick right on to a rocky, dirt path. I focus on the road ahead, which is very narrow. Thoughts begin to bombard my head about how serious this situation is. It's obvious that only one car can take this road at a time so wherever they are taking me, there are agents there that know we are coming. I also think about how long this is going to take. Joseph told me specifically what to say, and I intend on doing that quickly so this whole ordeal can be over as soon as possible. As the trees on both sides of the car become more and more dense I turn around again to check for headlights, trembling, hoping Joseph's headlights will cast some light into the car soon, just to give me a sliver of peace. Within moments some light bounces off the dash board. I turn around to see the black sedan Joseph is driving. I continue to glare at the road ahead, to see if anything is manifesting in the throng of trees. Then, I notice Sylvester retrieving his cell phone from the console. As he holds it up to his ear I can hear a voice coming from the other side.

A lady's voice beams, "Are you in the vicinity?"

Sylvester replies promptly, "Yes, Ma'am, we are one minute out."

Then, he hangs up. Just as he hangs up, Baynes makes a quick left and as soon as he completes the turn, I see it. It is a robust building that stretches the span of maybe one hundred yards and it stands three stories tall. The building is completely cinder block, like a prison, but the top floor is made of all glass windows. Because of the third floor having nothing but windows, it casts a bright spectrum of light over the land that it sits on. As we pull up to the building, I notice that there are four armed agents standing at the single door entrance of the facility, all of which are dressed in the same black and navy blue suits. The car stops and Baynes approaches my door to open it.

"Ms. Peterson," he says in a serious and surprising tone, and gestures for me to get out. I am irritated at the new demeanor these two now have, but I get out of the car and notice that Joseph is already standing at the entry way. I am escorted toward the entrance and the other four agents fall in line right behind us. Joseph cuts his eyes in my direction and I meet his gaze very briefly. He then slides a card on a side panel near the door. The panel makes a buzz, then Joseph places his thumb on the panel and a computerized voice says, "Welcome Agent Peters." I smirk at the sound of it because up until this point I had never noticed how similar our last names are. He looks back at me and we share a brief smile. The door opens and we all walk down a long white hallway. The floors are a sparkling white and they are buffed to perfection, so much so that you can see your reflection. The brightness of the long hallway makes the whole situation even more intense. Hearing the clacking echo of all of the agent's shoes, as we walk, begins to disturb me. The six agents surrounding me seem to double with the sound of the echoes in the empty hallway. The seriousness of the whole situation is baffling and I ponder why it is necessary to have six agents to handle an eighteen year old girl. *Father, I know you are with me where ever I go.*

After turning several corners, we finally reach a door. Joseph goes through the same procedure to open this door and again I smirk at the sound of his last name. I make an attempt to start a conversation to calm my nerves.

"Wow, this is weird."

Joseph looks over his shoulder, "What's weird?"

"That our last names are so similar," I reply.

"Oh, yeah," he responds sharply.

Joseph seems nervous too, and I can tell that his mind is somewhere else. I wait for Slyvester and Baynes to laugh at my juvenile revelation, but they don't; they are still maintaining their fake/serious demeanor. The door opens and I am perplexed that we enter an elevator. The elevator takes us up to the third floor. We exit the elevator and we are met by a tall, dark-haired woman, dressed in a navy blazer and a black pencil skirt. She is thin and strikingly beautiful. Her hair is pinned up with every piece of hair perfectly placed. The four agents split up, two on her right side and two on her left. Baynes and Sylvester have disappeared from view and my eyes dart around looking for them, but I am drawn back in when I hear the woman give Joseph orders, "Your services aren't needed anymore, Peters, you may go." Then she looks at me, and I notice her eyes are dark as coal and her thick eyebrows and lashes are accented by her dark red lipstick. Her dark features make her look attractive, but there is also a disturbing feeling about her. Her strong facial features are accentuated by her pale white skin and sharp bone structure. Joseph looks as though he is going to speak, but gives me a reassuring look that tells me he is not going far. As she leads me into a glass door on my left, I look over my shoulder at Joseph and to my dismay he is entering the elevator door. "This way, Ms. Peterson," the woman says with a demanding tone.

Once I enter the room I am flabbergasted at what I find. The room is shaped like a lowercase t. It is encompassed with windows on the opposite sides of the room. The right and left sides of me are where the windows give off a view of dense forestry at every angle. As I turn three hundred and sixty degrees, to take in my surroundings, I notice that the woman is still standing near the glass door, silently. I also notice that there's a large mirror to my right. This sets off a different wave of emotions, *a two way mirror*. She is watching me intensely. I meet her stare. She purses her lips and walks over to a steel table that sits in the center of the room. Once I notice the table, I notice two other things: the manila folder that is placed in the center of the table and a small white cot not too far away. She pulls out one of the chairs that occupy the table, and gestures for me to have a seat. I sit down. When she sits down she focuses her attention on the contents of the folder. I observe her serious demeanor, wondering what she could possibly be looking at is what concerns me. As I sit waiting, with my hands folded on top of the table, I fixate on her bold red lipstick, how perfectly it is applied and how she kind of reminds me of the lady on the World War II, "We Can Do It," propaganda posters.

Finally, after a few moments of flipping through the papers in the folder, she looks up.

"Miss. Peterson, the reason we have summoned you here today is to gain an understanding of how you got the information about the catastrophic events that have occurred in the past few days. I understand that you submitted this information to a local magazine a few weeks before the occurrences?"

Anxiously I reply, "First of all, I did not *give* that information to anyone, and secondly, I am not sure what you mean when you say, 'how I got the information'."

Pursing her lips, she leans back, folds her arms across her chest and says, "Yes, how did you get this information?"

I think back to what Joseph and I rehearsed, which is the truth, nothing more, nothing less.

"Well, I dreamt about it. Then I decided to write it down, and once I told a friend about it he stole my journal and took it to *The Spark*."

The women doesn't change her position, she looks directly into my eyes and asks, "Is there more to this dream?" she unfolds her arms, leans forward and begins to flip through the papers in the folder again. "It seems that the transcribed version of your dream is incomplete."

Trying not to be deceptive I reply, "That was all I could remember at the time."

She leans back again, folding her arms across her chest once again, she says, "Well."

"Well, what?" I retort.

"What was the rest of the dream?"

I search my mind for the rest of the script Joseph and I rehearsed. To my dismay there's only one more line, of which I am positive won't stop this interrogation.

"There isn't anything else. I woke up after the earthquakes happened. That's why it seems incomplete—because it is. I woke up on purpose. I didn't want to see the rest."

This isn't a lie because I did wake up on purpose and I didn't want to see the rest—I guess it is deceptive, but there is a time and place for everything. This is definitely not the time to reveal the rest of this dream.

The woman stands up abruptly. She walks over to the window with her arms still folded across her chest. For what seems like five minutes, I wait. Hoping to hear her say, 'Okay, you can leave now.' Those words don't come. She turns around, walks over to the table, picks up the folder and approaches the door that we entered the room through.

I stand up, "Well, can I leave now, you know, since there isn't anything else to tell?"

With her back still toward me she says, "Your presence here is indefinite, until you remember or dream the rest of what happens."

And in the blink of an eye, she leaves and the door shuts with a loud doomful thud. Reality sinks in; I am never leaving this place unless I reveal the rest of my dream. At this point the features of the room become more evident. This is somewhat of a cell with windows. I begin to take in the surroundings even more. The single person cot in the corner registers in my peripheral vision. I turn and look at it, then I look to my left and my right which is nothing but windows. They span the ceiling and continue down to the floor. All around me there are sounds. The sounds aren't people, but sounds of animals and nature. A dim light begins to penetrate the room and the lights that were illuminating the room turn off automatically. I walk over to the glass and gaze up at the sky and what should be a bright midnight blue by this time of the morning is a dim gray. As I continue to look up at the sky I realize it is about to start raining again and at that moment a flash of lightning brightens the landscape. I immediately recognize this image. It seems like a moment of Déjà vu. I continue taking all of the images in with the sounds and then it hits me. I realize where I am and where I have seen these images before.

Chapter 21

*S*itting here, all I can do is replay the haunting dream that has plagued me since I was a child. My stomach is in knots and all I can do is pray. I ask God for answers: why am I here, what do they expect from me, why did He give me a dream so soon before the actual events would take place. To occupy myself and to rid my thoughts of the confusion, I sit nestled in a corner. I stare out the window, counting the number of cars that come down the path; five is the number I end up with after what seems like hours of sitting in this position. There's a light shower beginning to come down and every so often I hear thunder rumbling through the clouds. Someone slips food into a compartment on the door and I don't lay a figure on it. I can't eat. My mind is on a million other things and food is not one of them. Time continues to tick by and I begin to think about Daniel and how distorted my image of him is now. I wonder if he regrets what he has done to me, or even thinks about me the same way I think about him. Then, I worry about my mom, whether or not she is concerned about me. She has come a long way in the past few months and I would hate for her to revert back to that slumber she basked in for so long. Finally, I begin to think about Joseph, how he has been with me through a large majority of this chaos. The entire country is in an uproar and he has yet to show any sign of discouragement or worry about the whole situation. He's such a solid example of how to cast your cares to God. Then, it dawns on me. Where is he? Why hasn't he come to see me? My hearts starts to beat a little faster. That feeling of despair begins to infiltrate my stomach again, just as it did the night of my graduation. The rain starts to fall harder, and I can now hear the drops hitting the roof. The paved road that the cars travel on becomes dark with mud and suddenly I see a large four door, gray Buick coming down the path. *Six*, I say to myself. It pulls into a parking space, two gentlemen get out, and the man on the passenger side walks around to the driver's side passenger door. He opens the door and a man in a fedora hat and a khaki trench coat steps out of the vehicle. When he begins to walk, I notice his hair. I rise to my feet to get a closer look. *It is him*. My stomach begins to churn, and I feel as though I am losing my balance. I place both of my hands on the glass to steady myself. I blink several times to see if maybe I am hallucinating because of how much I have been through, or maybe it's the room that is making me see these things. I continue to look and once the man is almost to the front door of the building he stops, as if he knows he has an audience, he looks in my direction, but doesn't make eye contact. "It *is* him," I say, out loud. I back away from the windows slowly until my back touches the door that is maybe twenty feet across the room. Trying to catch my breath, I remember that this man is not only familiar because of the dream, but he is also the owner of *The Spark*. I begin to feel as though I am going to have another anxiety attack, but then I hear some voices coming up the hallway. In an attempt to try to get my thoughts together and steady my breathing, I realize that one of the voices I hear is Joseph's. Then, in an instant, my fear turns into rage. Yeah, he is the owner of *The Spark*. He is the man that shook my hand and fought like crazy in court to get my premonition published. My heart rate increases even more. The voices get even closer, but I still can't make out what they are saying. Joseph knows about my ever present dream, and he also knows that this man was part of the reason I fainted on the street that day, but does he know he is here? When the voices seem to be right outside the door, I back away about ten feet. *Father, I know you are with me,* I mumble under my breath, *you have not given me the spirit of fear but of...,* the door opens. To my surprise Joseph enters abruptly and the door slams behind him. I am so happy to see him, I run to embrace him. He puts his arms around me and holds me tight, so tight that I can feel his heart beating against my cheek. His heart is beating just as fast as mine.

"Oh Joseph, I am so glad you are still here," I mumble.

"Did you really think I would leave you here? I have been trying to cut every corner I could to get you out of here."

I pick my head up slightly from his chest, just enough to look in his eyes.

"Are they going to let me go home?" I sob out.

With his eyes full of regret, as he loosens his arms to hold my face, he looks at me sharply, "Naomi, they have orders from the CIA to keep you here until they arrive to question you. The FBI has called in the owner of *Spark* to see if he could get you to talk. They don't want the CIA involved. They want to handle this case on their own. Naomi—" he pauses for a moment, "they want to keep you here until you dream again, until you can tell them what is going to happen next or give them an explanation of how you knew this would happen."

I pull away from him and reassume my position by the windows. I look out into the landscape hoping for answers, hoping God would show me a way to get out of this mess I am in. Why did he have to do it? Why did that idiot, Daniel, have to do this to me, I ponder. If he had never stolen my journal this would have never happened. The earthquakes would have occurred and no one would have ever known that I knew about them beforehand. Joseph comes up behind me and embraces me tightly.

He kisses my head softly and says into my hair, "I will get you out of here, Naomi. I promise."

I remain in his grasp and turn around to face him, "But how…"

I barely have time to finish my question when the woman from earlier walks in followed by someone else. I can't see who the person is, but I hear an extra set of footsteps.

"Okay, Agent Peters, you may leave now."

Joseph kisses me on the forehead and whispers, "I promise."

He obediently turns around and leaves the room. I'm gazing down at the floor when I hear the woman's footsteps are headed for the door, as well. The sound of the heavy door closing startles me and I quickly look up. I am faced with a real, living, breathing representation of the man who has been present in my dreams for years. He smirks a little, just as he did the first time I met him face to face. He walks over to the table in the center of the room and pulls out a chair for me to sit down. As stiff as a board I stand there, unwilling to move.

"What do you want with me?" I ask courageously.

"Aren't you going to sit down first?" he says with his awful screechy voice.

"No," I retort. "I would rather stand."

Truthfully I want to stay as far away from him as I can. I glance over to my left and stare at the double mirror. I look myself over for a moment and realize that this is the first time I have seen my reflection in days. My hair is a bee hive of fuzzy coils and my skin is a pale yellow. When he notices my attention is no longer on him, he clears his throat and sits down. I fix my eyes on a spot on the tile, vowing to not make eye contact. I begin to speak before he can get a chance to.

"Look, my dream ended after the earthquakes. I willed myself awake because the dream was very terrifying. I don't know what else you all expect me to do or say."

He sits calmly looking directly at me, as far as I can tell. He speaks tranquilly as if I did not just make a statement.

"Ms. Peterson, I am here to offer you an alternative. If you agree to publishing the rest of your dream in my magazine, this will all go away. You could go home and continue living your life, with a half million dollars."

For a quick second I jerk my head up in disgust, and at the sight of him I immediately resume focusing in on the small, dull, imperfection on the tile.

"You mean to tell me that you are going to bribe me into telling you something that I never dreamt. How would you know I am telling the truth?"

He begins to laugh loud and hysterically, "I know it will be the truth because I know you wouldn't want the entire country to go into a further state of mayhem."

I realize that this man is serious and seriously out of his mind. He carries on laughing as if this is a joke.

Finally, while he is still laughing, I retort in a very loud and serious voice, "Look, I don't know what to tell you. That was the entire dream and no amount of money is going to make me tell you something that can cause this country any more horror. Why don't you read the Bible? It can tell you everything you need to know." He stops laughing after the very last word leaves my lips.

With a hateful tone he says, "Well I guess you will rot here until you dream the rest of it."

He gets up abruptly, pushes his chair in, knocks at the door twice, and just like that, he is gone. I let out a huge breath and the floor seems to rise beneath me. As I hold myself up by grasping my knees, I realize that he wasn't so scary after all.

჊

There's no clock in the room, so it's difficult to keep track of time when the sky has been gray all day. Suddenly the dim night lights click on and I realize that it has gotten darker outside. I listen to steps and voices go up and down the hallway as I lie on the cot. I lay thinking of what to do next. Hours pass and it's now pitch black outside. The lights in my room clicked off maybe an hour or two ago and that lets me know that it is probably past nine p.m. I refuse to go to sleep in this place and I wonder if them holding me here like this is illegal. Soon I hear footsteps coming down the hall again. I know from the sound that it's not the woman, but a man's footsteps. I listen to them get closer and then they fade just like they have been doing all day. A few moments later, I hear voices that seem pretty close. I get up from the cot and walk over to the door to see if I can make out what is being said, but the voices are muffled. I put my ear on the door and suddenly the voices stop. Now I am hearing something that sounds like buttons on a telephone are being dialed. I hear a loud click, like the door is being unlocked and in an instant the door slides open and I fall forward. I am caught by whoever has unlocked the door and immediately I know who it is by the pleasing aroma that comes from his shirt, *Joseph*! I look up.

"Shhh," he says. "No one knows I am here, but the guard who is on duty."

I begin to whisper, "So what's your plan?"

He walks quickly to the windows and looks down at the cars on the compound. "Medusa just left, so it's a good a time as any to get you out of here."

"What do you mean 'get *me*' out of here? Aren't you coming with me?" I ask as I walk to the window to stand beside him. "And is her name really 'Medusa'?" I smile for the first time in the past few days.

"Nah, we just call her that behind her back. Agent Castro is her name, but we all loathe her presence and she just as well may be a demonic creature with the torment she bestows on us around here."

I give him a side look, "You didn't answer my first question."

"I know," he moves swiftly to the door again and sticks his head out. He looks to the left and to the right. "Although they are holding you, per-the CIA, you are not a criminal."

"Okay, what does that mean and what does that have to do with you coming with me?"

He quickly walks back over to me and grabs me by my arms. "That means, since you are not a high profile criminal they aren't many guards around. You are harmless. The guard that they have guarding you tonight is a very close friend of mine. He went on his security checks of this floor, and he agrees that he didn't see me come into your room tonight."

"What about the cameras?" I blurt out.

Joseph speaks quickly and in a whisper, "I have friends in the audio and camera room, as well. Now come on. We have to leave right now if you want to make your flight."

He lets go of my arms, takes my hand and guides me slowly to the door.

Again I ask, "What about you?"

Now turning to face me he says, "You have to leave on your own. I will catch up with you after I cover our tracks. We have to get you out of the country until this all dies down."

That settles it. I stop asking questions and follow Joseph out into the long, empty corridor. We walk several steps to our right and I recollect that we are going down the elevator. Once in the two by three foot space, where the elevator receives passengers, we hear voices coming up the hallway we just came from. My stomach drops and we press our backs up against the wall hoping that they will pass us and not attempt to board the elevator. The voices get closer and closer. Joseph braids his fingers through mine and squeezes my fingers tightly. His chest and mine go up and down in harmony as the voices get even closer. Then, we hear a third voice call to them, the voices sound like they are now standing right next to us.

"Hey, did you guys sign out?" another voice rings out.

Joseph looks over at me with a sigh of relief. The two people retreat in the direction they came and continue their conversation. Once their footsteps seem to be further down the hallway, the elevator dings. As I wait for the doors to open, I pray that no one is in the elevator. I close my eyes as the doors open. Joseph pulls me inside. In the forty-five second ride to the first floor, Joseph shares with me that the person who saved our butts was another rookie named James. He works in the surveillance room and must have seen the other agents coming down to board the elevator. Once we reach the first floor, there's another two by three space that we stand in. With our backs against the elevator door, Joseph quickly checks to see if anyone is in the foyer. He whispers, "It's clear." We walk maybe twenty steps to the front entrance, and I see Joseph give the camera facing the inside of the foyer a thumbs up. Every step we take I feel a weight lifting off of my back. Now inside the car, I feel even lighter and a smile creeps up on my face. Joseph looks over at me with a smile to match mine and says, "Don't get too excited yet. We still need to get out of this clearing and back on to the highway." Once on the dirt path that is still muddy from the rain, Joseph drives about forty-five miles per hour. I can tell that he is panicking because this is the only road in and out of the compound. After five miles of praying to God that we don't run into anyone, we reach the intersection of the path and the road. Joseph waits for a few cars to pass before he makes the right turn, but the third car slows down. Joseph looks over at me and I at him. He says, "GET DOWN!" I duck just as soon as the first syllable comes out of his mouth. He slowly makes the turn hoping that the passengers of the vehicle didn't notice me. Joseph drives calmly making sure he is going the speed limit and I ask, "Can I get up now?"

"Yeah, I don't think they noticed."

I sit up and turn to look behind us. There's nothing but pitch black scenery following us.

After a few moments pass I ask, "So where are you sending me?"

Joseph keeps his eyes on the road, "Don't say it like that."

"Like what? I mean, you *are* sending me somewhere."

He exhales, "Your mom and me planned it all out this evening. I went to the house to reassure her that you were fine and they just wanted to keep you for questioning. I let her know that they couldn't keep you more than twenty-four hours, but I wasn't sure what laws would have been pushed with Medusa heading this whole operation." He cuts his eyes at me. "We bought you a one-way ticket to London. You should be safe there until this whole situation dies down."

Frustrated, I start shooting as many questions at him as I possibly can, "Well, what do I do when I get there, what do I do for money, how do I get around, I don't know anyone in LONDON!"

I am hyperventilating at this point, confused and angry that they have basically done all of this without my consent.

"Naomi," He pats my back as I lean forward to catch my breath, "You will be fine, your mom and I have packed you a bag with everything you need; an account number with enough money in it to take care of you for several months, and your passport. We have a car that is supposed to pick you up when you land and take you to the hotel that we have reserved for you. You will be fine. I will come to check on you once I tie up the loose ends here."

My breathing slows and I ask another question, "How did you two get all of this done?"

Josephs smiles, but never takes his eyes off the road, "Haven't you noticed yet?" and in his familiar arrogant voice he says, "I have connections."

Chapter 22

O nce we reach the airport Joseph reaches over the seat to retrieve a blue book bag and gives me some instructions. "Okay," he exhales. "Put this hat on and this jacket. Don't start a conversation with anyone. Agents tend to blend in with the crowd and it is important not to blow your cover. Don't tell anyone your real name and don't try to contact your mom, Emmy, *Daniel,* or me. I will get in touch with you as soon as I can. There are some letters in the inside pocket of the jacket, from your mom and Emmy—don't try to read them until you are in flight. Everything else you need is in the backpack." He hastily opens his car door and just before I reach to open mine he says, "Oh yeah, there is also a small brown envelope in the bag with some spending money. Try not to spend it all in one place." He finally makes eye contact with me and smiles gingerly. We both exit the car and head for the European terminal. I pull the blue cap down snuggly on my head, tucking in any stray hairs. As we enter the sliding doors it begins to drizzle slightly. We retrieve my ticket and head for the Amtrak; it is apparent that my flight is boarding soon because Joseph is practically dragging me through the busy Atlanta airport. Just before we board the train that will take us to my gate, I hear a familiar voice yell, "Agent Peters!" Joseph looks quickly over his shoulder and breaks out into a full sprint for the train door. "Come on!" he yells. I begin to run catching up with him as he slows down for me. I suddenly recognize the voice that called his name. It's the woman, Agent Castro. *How did she find us, how did she know we were here?* I ask myself. Joseph continues running, looking back to see if she is running after us. I take a peek over my shoulder and catch a glimpse of the two male agents, Slyvester and Baynes, hot on our trail. I turn back around swiftly, now thanking God for the busyness of the airport. Joseph and I dodge an elderly couple being careful not to push them down, but we trample over a teenage couple holding hands, saying excuse me as we glide through the crowd. Joseph yells, "It's just up here, Naomi. We are going to have to part ways. Get on the train and run for gate twenty-three." Still running, I catch a glimpse of his face. He is flush red and all I can think about is how much I have to say; I want to express things that I haven't had a chance to say yet. I reach the train and in a blink of an eye the door opens, I board along with Joseph. I turn to look at him as the audio voice rings out, "This train is departing in thirty seconds." He grabs me by my face and presses his nose against mine. His breathing is rapid, just as mine is. He says to me in the midst of it all, "I love you, Naomi," and kisses me softly. Just like that, he's gone. In utter shock I watch him as the train departs and the two agents finally catch up to him. I watch as they pull him by both his arms, roughly, and the image fades as we enter a long dark tunnel.

ᔓ

Just as Joseph instructed me, I sprint for gate twenty-three and check in. I board the plane just in time. I squeeze my way through several passengers, placing their bags in the overhead-carriers, to find my seat. I am seated next to the window and for now, the seat beside me is empty. I place the backpack Joseph gave me between my legs to inspect its contents. Inside I find three maybe four outfits, another pair of shoes and my favorite snack, Twizzlers. My mom must have packed this bag, I think. Then I feel deep down in the bag for the small envelope that Joseph said would be there. It is there, and as I pull my hand back up through the bag I feel something else. I grab a hold of it to pull it out. My journal! I shout internally. I hold it to my chest, so grateful that my mom packed it for me. For a slight instance I question how she got into the safe, but I cast that thought away, grateful that I have it. My neighbor for the extensive flight finally arrives and I am grateful that it is an older women. She looks to be around my mom's age with long blonde hair, tinged with a gray hair here and there. She is slender and has a pleasant demeanor. She smiles at me as she takes her seat.

"Hello," she says, smiling even harder. "Taking a long trip by yourself like me, huh?"

"Yes," I respond returning a smile in her direction.

I stop there, because I remember Joseph telling me not to make conversations.

She continues as she takes her seat, "Well, I am visiting my two grandchildren. I am so excited to see them."

She looks over at me, waiting for a response, but I just smile gently at her, place my journal back at the bottom of my bag and adjust myself in my seat. I gaze out the window, watching the rain drizzle down. I reflect on the words that Joseph whispered to me several moments ago, *I love you, Naomi.* As the words cascade through my mind, I feel a warm sensation run through me. I close my eyes to catch a glimpse of his precious face once more. *He said he loved me.* At that moment I am reminded of the letters. *The letters!* I reach into the side pocket of the jacket and retrieve two letters. I go to open the first one, which is from my mom. I notice that it is very brief.

> *Hey baby girl,*
> *I know this is all a very sudden thing, but you are in good hands. Joseph seems to be very responsible and there is no doubt in my mind that he cares about you. I*

realize that you didn't get that opportunity to read the letter your Aunt Destine left for us, but I will see you soon and we will share it together. Be strong baby girl.

Love,
Momma

P.S. I know you are probably thinking, how did she get my journal out of the safe? Ask Joseph, he is very good at what he does.

I giggle to myself, disturbing the sweet lady who is sharing this space with me. She glances over briefly and giggles too, as if she knows what I am giggling about. As I am opening the second letter I feel the plane starting to move. The captain comes over the intercom.

"Hello Everyone, I am going to be your captain for this flight. We should have a smooth flight with light rain for the first few hours."

I listen as I hold the open letter in my hands. He continues on to let us know where we are going and what time we should land. Once he finishes, I fix my eyes on the text. Right away I recognize the handwriting.

Naomi,

I am not sure this letter will ever get to you, but I needed to write to you even though you may not ever read this. I asked Emmy to be sure that you get it. First of all, I am sorry for everything I have put you through. My judgment has been very clouded lately, but there is no excuse for what I have done. I hope you can forgive me because like you have always said, 'forgiveness is the first step to healing.' You are the epitome of love for me. I don't know how I am going to

live without you, but I pray one day you will forgive
me and we can at least be friends. I wish you all the
best Naomi. I love you and always will.

Daniel

Stunned that Emmy and Daniel even made contact *and* that she would even do something like this for him, I fold the letter back perfectly and place them both in the inside pocket of my jacket. I lean back in the seat and adjust my head to gaze out of the window. I feel the plane lift beneath me and before I know it, I am asleep, dreaming, dreaming of someone familiar carrying me and me whispering goodbye to a boy with golden straw-like hair.